≠
Sch67n

Northern Fried Chicken

Also by Roni Schotter
A Matter of Time

Northern Fried Chicken

Roni Schotter

P H I L O M E L B O O K S
New York

The author and Philomel books would like to thank the following for permission to reprint excerpts from songs and speeches in this book. All possible care has been taken to trace the ownership of every selection included and to make full acknowledgment for its use. If any errors have accidentally occurred, they will be corrected in subsequent editions, provided notification is sent to the publishers:

The American Jewish Congress, for excerpts from the address by Rabbi Joachim Prinz at the March on Washington in August 1963.

The Central Conference of American Rabbis, for material from *The Union Prayer Book I,* copyright © 1941, Central Conference of American Rabbis. Reprinted by permission.

Joan Daves, for excerpts from "I Have a Dream" by Martin Luther King, Jr., copyright © 1963 by Martin Luther King, Jr. Reprinted by permission of Joan Daves.

Ludlow Music, Inc., for "We Shall Overcome," by Zilphia Horton, Frank Hamilton, Guy Carawan and Pete Seeger. Copyright © 1960 and 1963, Ludlow Music, Inc., New York, New York. Reprinted by permission of Ludlow Music, Inc.

Sanga Music Inc., for "I Ain't Scared of Your Jail" by Lester Cobb, copyright © 1963, Sanga Music Inc. and "If You Miss Me at the Back of the Bus" by Carver Neblett, copyright © 1963, Sanga Music Inc. Reprinted by permission of Sanga Music Inc.

Warner Bros. Music, for "Puff the Magic Dragon" by Peter Yarrow and Leonard Lipton, copyright © 1963, Pepamar Music Corp. Reprinted by permission of Warner Bros. Music.

Except for historical persons and events, the characters
and situations in this book are entirely fictional.

First published in 1983 by Philomel Books, a division of The Putnam Publishing Group, 51 Madison Avenue, New York, NY 10010.

Copyright © 1983 by Roni Schotter
First edition.
Designed by Jacqueline Schuman

Library of Congress Cataloging in Publication Data
Schotter, Roni.
    Northern fried chicken.
    Summary: A Jewish high school girl becomes increasingly involved in human rights for blacks in the early 1960s at the cost of some other important relationships in her life.
    [1. Afro-Americans—Civil rights—Fiction. 2. Jews—United States—Fiction. 3. Friendship—Fiction]
    I. Title.
PZ7.S3765No 1983   [Fic]   83-2459
ISBN 0-399-20920-4

The author gratefully acknowledges the help of the following people and organizations: Marie F. Harper, reference librarian at the Rhode Island Historical Society; D. Louise Cook, director, King Library and Archives at the Martin Luther King, Jr., Center for Nonviolent Social Change, Inc.; John Bucci, reference librarian, and Ruth D. Jones, cataloger, at Simon's Rock of Bard College Library; the American Jewish Congress; Central Conference of American Rabbis; Fran Chirch; Sally Goodis; Betty Jane Jacobs; Alfred Litman; Jeanne Siegel; and Steve J. Zipperstein

For Richard,
Precious Friend

Author's Note

Northern Fried Chicken is the story of Betsy Bergman, and although it is fictional, it takes place in a very real time. The 1960s were an era of great change. One hundred years had passed since Abraham Lincoln had freed the slaves and yet, black Americans still were not truly free.

In some states, especially in the south, black people were not free to go to the same movie theaters or eat at the same restaurants or swim at the same beaches as white people. At lunch counters and on buses and trains, they were forced to sit apart from white people. Poll taxes and various forms of intimidation kept them from registering to vote. And black students were often prevented from attending the same schools and universities that white students attended.

In other states, especially in the north, *de facto* segregation, a less obvious form of discrimination, was common. Although black people were supposedly treated equally, this was often not the case. Job discrimination kept most black people poor. Discrimination in housing forced many black families to live separately from white people and their children to attend second-rate schools where they had less opportunity to learn than white students.

But, beginning on a large scale in 1960 and continuing through the Sixties, black people and white people of every religion began the freedom rides and sit-ins, the marches and demonstrations that attempted to change this awful reality.

It seemed as if everything was changing in the Sixties, even language. In *Northern Fried Chicken,* Charlayne refers to herself as "Negro" as did most black people of that time. But as the Sixties unfolded, more and more people of Afro-American descent began to call themselves "black," just as Caucasian Americans call themselves "whites." In the late Sixties, when the civil rights movement reached its height, the word "black" became the preferred term, and by 1967 or so, Charlayne would probably have been proudly calling herself black.

Many years have passed and many tragic events have taken place since then. Some things have changed for the better. Some have not. But the struggle of human beings for their freedom and dignity continues.

R.S.

Northern Fried Chicken

1

Mayflower Avenue was half asleep as I struggled up the long hill in my new spike heels. It was one of those autumn mornings in late September when the air smells spicy, cold, and mysterious. I stopped for a moment to inhale the tangy aroma of earth, wood, and wet leaves, but all I could think of was the pain in my pinched toes. Ignore your feet, I told myself and try to walk like a lady—like Bernie. But it was impossible. With every step I thought about how stupid highheels were and how much sooner I could get to Bernie's house if only I was wearing my loafers.

Bernie lives around the corner from me on Edgeware Road. But because our streets form the city line, Bernie lives in Providence, Rhode Island, and I live in Pawtucket, Rhode Island—close, but worlds apart.

Mayflower Avenue is a jumble of tiny new one- and two-family houses, bicycles, screaming kids, and yelping dogs. But Edgeware Road is different. Quiet, old, and elegant, it's the kind of place that makes you think of china teapots, wood fires, and good posture.

I straightened my shoulders. In front of me was Bernie's house. The wind sent leaves soaring over the gray roof like brilliant-colored birds. I walked down the long gravel driveway to the back entrance, threw my weight against the heavy wooden door, turned the brass handle, and pushed my way in.

"Bernie?" I yelled. Bernie's family had already left for synagogue and no one, not even Itzhak, Bernie's cat, answered. The house smelled sweet and thick— of furniture polish and floor wax.

"Bernie?" I called again. "Where are you?"

I walked across the gleaming linoleum and hurried up the backstairs to her room.

When I opened the door, there was no sign of Bernie—all I could see were clothes: clothes tumbling out of drawers; clothes luxuriating on chairs; clothes clutching onto doorknobs; clothes lying exhausted on the floor. Bernie's bed was barely visible. In all the years that we've been best friends, I've never seen her blanket. I'm not even sure if she has one.

"Okay, Bernie," I said in my tough-guy voice. "Come out with your hands up."

There was a strange muffled sound, Itzhak scooted out from behind a pile of underwear, then two bare feet poked out from under the bed.

"With you in a moment," Bernie answered. "Just have to locate my garter belt."

"For goodness' sake, Bernie, you're supposed to be dressed. My parents are picking us up in twenty minutes. Your folks will be furious if we're late."

" 'Mortified' is a more ap-pro-pri-ate word," Bernie said, slithering out from under the bed in her bra and panties. "*What* will Rabbi Dressler think?" Bernie asked, imitating her mother. "*Late* for Rosh Hashanah services!"

I brushed a robe, some rollers, and some pink baby-doll pajamas onto the floor and sat down on the chair across from Bernie's bed. "Happy New Year." I tossed my brown veil on the bed and kicked off my shoes. "What year is it anyway?"

"5723," Bernie answered, reaching, like a magician, into the center of the mound and pulling out a pair of stockings. "The first day of *Tishri* in the year 5723, otherwise known as September 29, 1962. *Leshanah Tovah Tikatevu.*"

"Excuse me?"

"May you be inscribed for a year in the Book of Life."

"Oh, thanks," I said, grinning at her. "May you inherit your father's goats."

"May *you* inherit my father's goat's good-looks." Bernie smirked and then headed for the bathroom.

"Hurry *up*," I giggled, but she had already disappeared.

I got up to poke around the room and noticed Bernie's new wool slacks draped across her desk, and, underneath them, a neatly hand-lettered sign that read:

FOOD FOR FREEDOM
a project of PROJECT,
The *Providence* *J*ewish *E*ducational
and *C*ultural *T*ask Force
Help Us Help Our Negro Neighbors in the South

"Bernie," I called. "This is great."

"What?" she shouted from the bathroom.

"The sign. It's so professional!"

"I know," she gurgled, brushing her teeth. "D'you fine-an-supermankit?"

"A *what??*"

There was a sound of spitting and then, "A su-per-mar-ket! Did you *find* one?"

"Oh . . . yeah. Finally! Almacs. They said we could do it as long as we stood outside. But I was so scared, Bernie. The manager at True Foods hung up on me. I was lucky the guy at Almacs was nice."

"You're always scared," Bernie yelled.

"I know," I said, feeling awful. "As soon as I'm finished with one thing, I'm afraid of something else."

"Well, what is it now?" Bernie stuck her head into the room. Toothpaste oozed from the corner of her mouth.

"I guess it's stupid, but the idea of standing outside that supermarket with a big sign asking people for food to send to Negro people down south makes me nervous. What if someone gets angry?"

15

"It'll be fun, Betsy. Don't worry about it. You think too much." She went back into the bathroom.

"You're not scared of *any*thing, are you, Bernie."

"What?"

"I said, are you scared of *anything?*"

"Hmmm . . . Nope. I guess I just don't think about things as much as you do. The only thing that scares me . . . is my parents."

"Yeah, I know what you mean," I said. Bernie's parents expect a lot from her: the right grades (A's), the right college (Pembroke), and the right dates (Jewish).

"Have you decided what you're going to wear when we go?" Bernie yelled to me.

"Wear?" I hadn't thought about it. "Clothes. Who cares?"

"Oh, Betsy, you *never* know who you might meet."

"Right. Martin Luther King on a tour of Providence. Maybe President Kennedy. Just passing through. You never know," I said in my most mocking voice. But Bernie was running the water again and either didn't hear me or else wouldn't admit that she did.

Bernie's always on the hunt for boys, or, as she calls them, "men." And, to spite her parents, she's usually on the hunt for "Christian men."

On Bernie's nightstand, next to a sexy photo of Fabian, was her *Union Prayer Book.* I picked it up and started flipping the pages. The Hebrew letters made a beautiful design, but I could barely read a word.

Religion has never been a big thing to me. It isn't that I don't *care* about being Jewish, it's just that I have trouble with the formal part of it.

Bernie's the one who knows about being Jewish. It's another thing her parents expect of her. They want Bernie to feel the same way they do about their religion. Deep inside, I knew Bernie already did, but you'd never guess it from the way she acted. For instance, her parents keep kosher and Bernie isn't allowed to eat bacon. Every once in a while, usually on Sundays, my mother cooks bacon for breakfast, and whenever Bernie's especially angry with her parents, she shows up to eat it. Bagels and lox and bacon and eggs. On the sly.

"What are you so busy contemplating?" Bernie was dressed and standing before me.

"Immoral meat. The mysteries of bacon. . . . Hey, you look great!"

In a few short minutes, Bernie had accomplished her magic. She wore a new blue pleated skirt, a lavender blouse she'd bought on sale at Peerless Company, and her sister Joan's old red wool jacket. As usual, it all worked beautifully together.

Standing next to her at the mirror in my old brown jumper and faded wool sweater, I decided I was just this side of invisible.

"What you need is some color," Bernie said, reading my mind. She yanked a copper-colored scarf from the pile of clothes at our feet and draped it around my neck, tying it neatly in back. Then she handed me a bag of makeup and turned away to apply her own. In the time it took for me to do my lipstick and mascara, she finished her entire face.

"You know what, Bernie?" I complained. "I hate this beauty business. You like it because you're good at it. But to me it's a pain."

"Oh, Betsy," Bernie said, pushing my head to one side and teasing a lump of hair until it blended with the rest, "don't start."

"But, Bernie," I said, feeling more and more angry, "it isn't fair! Boys don't have to go through all this junk. They just throw on some clothes, run a comb through their hair, and they're ready for the world. How come we . . ."

"Oh, Betsy," Bernie sighed. "When you aren't scared, you're angry! Close your little eyes and shut your big mouth." She reached for the hair spray. "I told you before, you think too much."

A heavy, sweet, nauseating smell filled my lungs and started me choking, but when I sprayed Bernie's hair, she just shut her eyes and smiled.

Out in the street a horn blasted. My parents had no sense of dignity or place. Maybe you sounded your horn on Mayflower Avenue, but on Edgeware Road you rapped gently on the door.

Outside, my sister Jeannie stood alongside the red Rambler waving her arms in huge circles like a half-crazed windmill. Last month Jeannie turned ten and ever since then she's been acting like a candidate for officer training school. She wrinkled her face like an oversize prune and made another set of gyrations that I took to mean "Get down here."

"Two minutes!" I shouted out the window at the top of my lungs—then slammed my hand over my mouth.

"*Eee*-liz-a-beth," Bernie said, imitating her mother again. "Kindly muzzle your mouth!"

I pulled my head back in the room and ran to get my veil. Bernie lifted a brand-new pillbox hat over her head and set it carefully into place. I plopped my veil on and ran to get my shoes.

Downstairs, the horn blasted again.

"Come on!" I called to Bernie, pulling on my spikes and half-skipping, half-stumbling down the stairs like an old drunk.

"Coming," Bernie called. She grabbed her prayer book, stepped into her spikes, and floated gracefully down behind me. Like a queen.

2

Although it was early, people had already begun to assemble outside Temple Israel. The more religious ones, like Bernie's parents, had walked. The rest had driven.

"Look at Mrs. Bernstein's hat," Bernie said. "It looks like a flying saucer just landed."

"Or a large pizza," I whispered.

Men and women stood in small groups greeting each other, smiling and self-conscious—anxious to speak to friends but aware of the solemnity and importance of the occasion. On the ten days following Rosh Hashanah, God is supposed to decide everyone's fate for the next year—whether to inscribe us for another year in the Book of Life or whether to punish us for our misdeeds. Between Rosh Hashanah and Yom Kippur, the Day of Atonement and the holiest day of the Jewish year, we are supposed to contemplate our sins and ask God and ourselves for forgiveness.

For me, Rosh Hashanah is simply an extra chance to make resolutions. An extra chance to think about what I've done wrong during the year and how I'd like to change.

"Look out, Bets—it's the man of your dreams," Bernie said breathlessly in her best Jacqueline Kennedy imitation. She raised her arm high in the air and waved.

"Stop it, Bernie!" I hissed. But it was too late. Kenny Klein

---

was headed straight toward us. A senior and the vice-president of PROJECT, for one full year I'd been wishing he'd ask me out.

"Bernie, I don't know what to say!"

"Say anything. Say hello. I know—tell him about Almacs. Tell him you got them to say yes."

"Hi, Betsy and Bernie." Kenny's blue eyes looked down at me and then at Bernie and suddenly I felt short of breath. "How's it going?"

I glanced at Bernie.

"Fine, Kenny, fine," she answered. I felt her elbow embed itself in the right side of my stomach.

"Yeah," I croaked. "Everything's fine, just fine."

"Well . . . great," Kenny said. He shifted his weight from one foot to the other. It was obvious that he wasn't exactly inspired by our conversation. "Guess I better go hunt up my parents. They're somewhere in this crowd. See you around, Betsy and Bernie. Happy New Year, Mr. and Mrs. Bergman . . . Jeannie."

My parents and Jeannie smiled. Kenny gave us a wave and then disappeared behind a group of people.

"What's the matter with you, Betsy? You didn't say more than five words to him!"

"Limited vocabulary, I guess." Why was it so easy to be clever when it didn't count?

"He likes you. I can tell by the way he smiles at you."

"At *me*, Bernie?" I said angrily. "No one ever smiles at *me*. They smile at *us*. It's always Betsy *and* Bernie. I might as well start signing my name Miss Elizabeth Ann Andbernie. The only reason anyone even remembers my name is because they know yours comes next."

"For goodness' sake, Betsy. You underestimate yourself."

I frowned at Bernie, but she was ignoring me now.

"Hadn't we better go in, Mr. and Mrs. Bergman?" She smiled graciously at my parents and swept us through the crowds and into the temple. "Levin," she whispered to one of the ushers inside. He waved us on toward the closed doors of the still-empty sanctuary. Empty, except for Bernie's mother and sister in aisle seats in a middle row and Bernie's father and two other men in long white robes, sitting on high-backed chairs on the pulpit.

A ray of early-morning sun shone through a window in the roof, spotlighting the pulpit as if it were a stage. The air was charged with expectation. Bouquets of white gladiolus fanned out in front of the rabbi's lectern and at various places on the pulpit. Everything had been scrubbed and polished until it gleamed. The flame of the Eternal Light flickered and glowed like a jewel in its red glass container. Behind a curtain of heavy, richly–colored fabric, the Scroll sat hidden in The Holy Ark, waiting.

Mrs. Levin and Bernie's sister, Joan, turned around in their seats and smiled at us; and from the pulpit, Dr. Levin nodded formally, a blue *yarmulke* hiding the balding spot at the back of his head.

Sitting on the pulpit is an honor even though it means sitting absolutely still and being stared at for the entire length of the service. But Bernie's father likes that sort of thing.

"He looks good up there," I said carefully.

"Not bad, I guess," Bernie said. But she was staring with what looked like admiration at her father.

"Happy New Year," Mrs. Levin whispered as we sat down. Joan said nothing.

The organ groaned, the doors to the sanctuary opened, and everyone filed down the aisles and into their seats.

From across the room, Janet Bloom waved to us.

"Well, look who's here! Wave, Betsy." Bernie's teeth clenched into a phony smile. "How do you think she found the time in her busy schedule to join us?"

"Oh, Bernie, that's not fair. She's nice," I said, thinking as I waved back how Bernie overdid the criticism bit. But then, I really didn't know Janet all that well and it certainly was true that she was always busy—even during summer vacations. This summer she went down south with her parents to work on the Voter Education Project, helping to register Negro voters. She was always friendly to me, but somehow I never felt comfortable with her the way I did with Bernie.

Behind us, Neil Segal, the president of PROJECT, whispered hello. Bernie snapped around in her seat, hiking up her skirt. "Hi, Neil," she said during a pause in the organ music, and her voice rang out across the room.

"Ber-niece!" Mrs. Levin glared and Bernie turned quickly around and lowered her head.

A side door opened and Rabbi Dressler entered wearing a white robe, matching skullcap, and an embroidered gold *tallis*. From above, the choir began singing the opening hymn.

Rabbi Dressler walked slowly to the lectern, gripped the edges of it, and paused to look out at us. The soft jumble of whispers, shifting feet, and prayer books opening faded as everyone looked back at him.

In a voice that hinted at his Eastern European background, he spoke softly and carefully as if pronouncing each word for the very first time. "Will you turn now in your prayer books to page forty-one and read with me. 'Almighty and merciful God . . .' " he began. After a few faulty starts, we all joined in. " '. . . who hast called our fathers to thy service, and hast opened their eyes to behold thy wondrous works . . .' "

"Hast thou a Kleenex?" I whispered to Bernie. My nose was running.

"Dost thou mind a used one?" Bernie asked. She reached into her jacket pocket and handed me something that looked like white shredded wheat. I blew my nose. My mother looked up and gave me a faraway smile. My father and Jeannie were absorbed in the service. So were Joan and Mrs. Levin. Soon even Bernie was. I counted thirty-five navy blue hats in the fifteen rows in front of me. Then I looked back at Rabbi Dressler.

"O Rock of Israel," he was saying with feeling, "redeem those who are oppressed and deliver those who are persecuted. . . ."

I thought about being oppressed and persecuted. I didn't

think I knew anyone who was, but then I remembered the Negro people.

Last spring, when I heard that Janet Bloom and her family were going down south, I'd felt excited and scared. Part of me wanted to go. When I asked my father, he hesitated for a moment and then told me I was too young. Secretly, I was relieved. But he was wrong. I wasn't too young to go—I was too afraid.

I looked up at the pulpit. Dr. Levin stood at the lectern and another man stood near him holding the ram's horn.

Bernie nudged me with a smirk on her face.

"Oh, cut it out," I whispered. I knew she was proud and I wished she could admit it this once.

"Te-Ki-ah!" Dr. Levin called out loudly, and the man next to him put the *shofar* to his lips, took a huge breath, and blew a long, disturbing note that ended abruptly. *"Shevarim,"* Dr. Levin called. The man with the ram's horn blew some broken notes. *"Teruah!"* Dr. Levin shouted, and a series of strange wavering sounds mixed with quick, short ones echoed across the synagogue.

The rest of the service passed by me in a haze. Somewhere in another world, Rabbi Dressler was delivering his sermon. I cleared my head and tried to concentrate.

"My colleagues, the Reverend A. Hinton Howland of the Benefit Street Episcopalian Church, the Reverend James Carter Thompson of the Central Presbyterian Church, along with many of my coreligionists, are asking our congregants to reflect upon the trials of our Negro brothers and sisters in the North as well as in the South. They are struggling today to obtain their freedom just as we Jews did long ago in Egypt. . . ."

The synagogue filled with tension. Instantly, everyone was paying attention, wondering what Rabbi Dressler would say next.

". . . Only four days ago Mr. James Meredith, a Negro citizen of the United States and a veteran of our armed forces, tried for the second time to enroll at the University of Mississippi.

And for the second time, he was denied entrance. He was forcibly barred from the campus by the governor of Mississippi himself, Mr. Ross Barnett. Why? Because Mr. Meredith's skin is brown and Mr. Barnett thinks he is higher than the Supreme Court, higher than the Lord himself."

There was some polite laughter mixed with much coughing. Bernie glanced nervously at me.

Two years before, Rabbi Dressler had been one of the first freedom riders. He had ridden a bus through the South with some Negro and white members of the Congress of Racial Equality. It was one of the first attempts to end segregation on buses and it was in all the papers. Many people thought that as a rabbi he should "stick to religion," but it seemed to me he was a hero.

"It is easy to point fingers and look disapprovingly at others, but first we must evaluate ourselves—*our* attitudes and actions. On this first day of the New Year, I want you to consider our brother, Mr. James Meredith, and to judge what your own attitudes and actions toward him might be. Do bigotry and persecution exist only in the South? Or are there any among us, any in this very room, who harbor injustice in their hearts? Psalm ninety-six says of the Lord, 'for he cometh to judge the earth; with righteousness shall he judge the world, and the people with equity.' I ask you now to judge yourselves. . . . Amen."

Everyone sat with head bowed in silent meditation. I wondered if I harbored injustice in my heart—if I was bigoted. All I knew was that I didn't have a single Negro friend. There was Charlayne Perry, but she wasn't a friend. She was just someone I knew. She had moved up north with her family this year from Georgia and she was in my Spanish class. She was nice and I liked her and could tell that she liked me, but I always felt shy around her. I didn't know what it was. She just seemed different. Was it fear or shyness or was it bigotry? Maybe Rabbi Dressler was right. Maybe I was one of the people in the room who harbored injustice in my heart. It was time to make my Rosh Hashanah resolution. This year I was finally going to stop being so frightened and shy. Like Bernie said, I had to stop thinking so much and start acting. I was glad I was doing the Food for Freedom thing. It was a first step.

"Stand up, Betsy," Bernie whispered. "He's doing the benediction."

I jumped to my feet and bowed my head.

"The Lord bless you and keep you. The Lord make his face to shine upon you and be gracious unto you."

There was a lot of murmuring as people turned to their neighbors to wish them well.

"*Leshanah Tovah Tikatevu,*" Mrs. Levin said to Bernie and me.

"Happy New Year," I said. I didn't know yet if it would be *happy,* but I was determined that it would be *new.*

3

"Are you sure you should go?" my mother asked me.

It was Monday afternoon and I had come into the kitchen to grab a snack before meeting Bernie to go to Almacs. The radio was on and my mother sat at the kitchen table surrounded by piles of books. She was educating herself again—poring through volumes with titles like *How To Make It in the Stock Market, Financial Security,* and *Understanding the Dow-Jones.*

"What?" I asked, though I'd heard her every word.

I knew exactly what she was thinking. The day before, President Kennedy had made a speech on television asking the students at the University of Mississippi to accept desegregation peaceably. But all through the night there had been rioting, and only this morning James Meredith, escorted by federal troops and U.S. marshals, had finally enrolled.

"You can never tell—maybe people up here feel the same way as people down there do—about Negroes. They could be unpleasant. Are you sure you should go?"

"Sure? Of course I'm sure," I said. But I slammed the door to the refrigerator. Why *was* it that whenever I was the least bit afraid of anything, my mother could always be relied upon to put words to my fears and make me even more afraid. Weren't parents supposed to reassure their kids? No wonder I had to make resolutions before I could act. No wonder it was so hard for me to do everything.

"The radio said two people were killed last night and hundreds were injured."

"That's Mississippi, mom. Not Rhode Island." But I wondered if things like that could happen in the North.

"Two, four, one, three. We hate Kennedy." The radio carried the angry chant of the students at Ole Miss right into the kitchen. I leaned over and changed the station. Sam Cooke was singing "Twistin' the Night Away." I switched off the radio. It was odd. While in one place people were chanting and others were fighting for their rights, in another, folks were singing and dancing. Then there was me, sitting comfortably in a kitchen eating. It didn't seem right.

"So what should I do, mom? Stay home? Do nothing? I sounded forceful and sure of myself, but my heart was beating rapidly and as usual part of me hoped she'd forbid me to go.

"Of course not," she said. "You know that's not what I meant. I just worry a lot. . . . I'm not as brave as you are. Here . . ." she said, getting up from the table. She opened the closet and pulled out a small carton of food—a few cans of tuna, some baked beans, some sardines, and a large tomato juice. "For the cause."

"Thanks." I smiled at her. "Great!" But I was thinking about what she'd said. If it was true that I was being brave for once, it was because of Bernie; her fearlessness was contagious. I took a swallow of milk and bit into a carrot. "What's all this financial stuff?"

"I'm trying to make us some money."

"What are you going to do? Sell a couple of shares of AT and T and parlay them into millions?"

My mother looked hurt. "Why not? It's about time I did something important. I've already spoken to Jerry Gitter and he said he would recommend some more-active stocks. In fact, he suggested that if I wanted, I could come down to the brokerage house and take a look around."

"At *what?*" I asked too loudly. For the last year or so, my mother had had what she called her "problem." I wasn't exactly sure what it was except that it was a vague feeling of sadness and boredom. This stock thing was beginning to sound like yet another of my mother's schemes to busy herself. "What is it that you're going to look at?"

"At the ticker tape, for one thing. . . . What's the matter with you, Betsy? You always seem to get angry with me whenever I try something new. Jeannie and you are pretty much grown up now. What am I supposed to do? Sit home and watch TV all day?"

"It's not that, mom," I said. "It's not that you start things, it's that you give up on them and then you're sadder than before." I thought of her last project. "What happened to returning to college and getting your degree?"

"But I told you what the admissions director said—"

"So what? So he didn't think you were serious. Who cares about him anyway? Why didn't you tell him to go—"

My mother was crying.

"I'm sorry," I said. "I'm really sorry. . . . It's easy for me to tell you what you should do, but if it were me, I couldn't do it either. I just wish you could be happy again."

"It's okay, and you're right about me, Betsy. I *don't* follow through. But this time, with the stocks, it's going to be different."

"I hope so," I said, looking out the window and wishing I could believe her.

"Hey, Betsy!" Jeannie came in the back door carrying a brown bag. "I stopped at the grocery on the way home from school and bought some stuff for your Food For Freedom thing."

"Really? That's neat of you. What did you get?"

"Three tins of smoked oysters and one of clams. I ran out of money."

"For goodness sake, Jeannie. What do you think they're doing down there? Giving cocktail parties?"

My mother glared at me. "Betsy, you're going to have to do something about your temper. You blow up too easily."

'Sorry, Jeannie. It's just that we're trying to collect staples—you know," I said, spelling it out, "supplies—things to keep them going."

"Then why don't you collect prunes? That'll keep them going." Jeannie stuck out her tongue, but I could see that she was hurt. "I just thought I should send them something I like."

"Well, then, how come you forgot spaghetti?" Jeannie adores spaghetti. Every Saturday morning she cooks herself a bowl for breakfast.

"I don't know. *I* like it, but it seemed too ordinary. . . . But wait! If *you* buy spaghetti, they could make it with clam and oyster sauce! That would be pretty special!"

Suddenly Jeannie was off in a pasta reverie. Her lips parted and I could hear her breathing pick up. She seemed to be in some sort of trance just thinking of all those workers down south cooking pots and pots of spaghetti with clam and oyster sauce.

"Okay, okay," I said. My mother was eyeing me, ready to pounce. "I suppose it's the thought that counts." I took the tins of oysters and clams and put them in the carton along with the stuff from my mother. I glanced at the clock and suddenly felt my nervousness returning. "I better go. Bernie's picking me up in a few minutes. I'm meeting her out front."

"Don't forget the spaghetti," Jeannie said.

"Be careful, Betsy," my mother added.

"Yeah," I said, grabbing my jacket. I picked up the carton and ran as fast as I could to the front of the house and out the door. I was afraid if I stayed one minute longer in that kitchen, I'd never leave.

The drive to Almacs takes roughly fifteen minutes if you stay within the twenty-five-mile-an-hour speed limit, but we made it, flying low in Bernie's parents' '59 Buick, in just under ten.

Bernie whisked us into the parking lot and pulled into a spot near the front. As soon as she switched off the motor, I started to perspire. And when I looked out the side window, my stomach turned over. This was too much. God had overheard my Rosh Hashanah resolution and had decided to test me. There, standing in front of the supermarket next to a shopping cart, was Charlayne Perry wearing two huge signs on her front and back that said:

> Baptist Youth Fellowship
> Food For Freedom.
> Bread Brings Votes.
> Please Help.

She'd already spotted me and was waving. I waved back and tried to calm the unsettled feeling in the pit of my stomach.

"Looks like we have company," Bernie said tightly. "Who invited *her?*" Bernie sounded especially nasty and I didn't need her voicing my innermost thoughts.

"Don't worry about it," I snapped, trying desperately to hold on to my temper.

"I'm not worried," Bernie said evenly. "I'm annoyed. Like my parents always say when I get on their nerves, 'Two's company. Three's a crowd.' "

"Bernie," I exploded. "Sometimes I think you're a first-class snob. Anti-social. You never have a good word to say about anyone. What's the matter? She taking up your space or something?"

Bernie said something, but I didn't stop to listen.

"I bet you think we're the only ones who should be allowed to help Negroes," I yelled. "Don't you think Charlayne has the right to help her own people? Well, let me tell you something. She *has* the right! Same as you. Same as me. *More!*"

I stopped and took a deep breath. I felt better, but I wished I could suck everything back inside again. Unfortunately, it was too late. I could hear and almost touch the raw silence in the car. Bernie wasn't making a sound, but I knew it was only a matter of long, slow seconds before she turned on me.

"Well," she began very slowly and carefully. "What have we here? Miss High-and-Mighty? Miss Holier-than-Thou? If you're so gung-ho, why are you still sitting here in the car? Why don't you jump right out and lend a helping hand? Or are you too chicken to do it without snobbish antisocial me?"

I didn't answer.

"You ever hear of southern fried chicken?"

I kept my mouth tightly closed.

"I asked you a question," Bernie yelled. "I said, you ever hear of southern fried chicken?"

I knew I had no choice. Bernie required assistance in my torture. I had to help her out. "Yeah. I've heard of it."

"Well, you know what you are?"

"What?" I asked miserably.

"*Northern* fried chicken. Miss Northern Fried Chicken, 1962. Just sitting there dripping with fear, eager to help her poor southern neighbors—"

31

"Bernie, stop! Please—" I started to cry. "I'm sorry."

Bernie just sat there. Her eyes were wet and she stared straight ahead. I stared at the dashboard, seeing but not seeing the glove compartment. Finally Bernie reached her hand out to grab mine, and in a moment we were hugging each other.

"I'm sorry, Bernie. It was just nerves and my lousy temper," I said. "What you said about me before. Either I'm scared or I'm angry. It's getting worse and worse. Sometimes I get so overloaded I can't control myself. But I didn't mean a word of it."

"Me neither, Betsy. I didn't mean a word of anything I said."

"Yeah-you-did," I said, "and what's more, it's true. But I wish you weren't so clever and right on target. *Northern fried chicken*—that's perfect! It's me," I said.

"No, it isn't," Bernie insisted. "You know how I get when someone criticizes me—I'll say anything. I didn't mean to be mean any more than you did. It's just that I thought it would be fun—the two of us—you know—Betsy and Bernie."

"It can still be fun, Bernie," I said quietly. "What difference does one person make?"

But then I thought that maybe I understood what was going on. As promised, Bernie was all dressed up. Wearing stockings and heels. Covered with makeup that was dripping in long, slow streaks down her face. And as usual, I was decked out in my old gray knee socks with the wool balls dangling from them, scuffed loafers, and my corduroy skirt with the grape-soda stain on the hem. I stared at Bernie for a few seconds, and for the very first time in all my years of knowing Bernie, I felt sorry for her.

"Bernie," I said gently. "Charlayne and I aren't any competition for you. If there are guys, they'll be be white and they won't go for Charlayne. If they're handsome, they won't go for me. And anyway, Charlayne's wearing her sign and I'll wear ours. You'll be the only girl anyone can see. . . . Is that it, Bernie? Is that what's bothering you?"

Bernie shrugged. "Part of it. Oh, Betsy, do you think I'm awful?"

"Nyah. Annoying, occasionally lethal, but . . ." I said, kissing her, " you're my best friend and I'll always love you. Now, please, let's get out of here. Miss Northern Fried Chicken has work to do."

5

Fifteen minutes later, I stood next to Charlayne by the door to the supermarket, my head peering over the top of Bernie's huge sign. I tried to smile and act casual, but I couldn't manage it. I was frightened and I knew I looked ridiculous. My knees shook, rattling the huge sign ever so slightly.

"Well," Bernie said, perfectly at ease. She was eyeing a silver-haired lady who had just exited from the supermarket. " 'If it were done when 'tis done, then 'twere well it were done quickly.' Shakespeare," she called to us over her shoulder as she strolled off in fearless pursuit. "Macbeth."

"Obnoxious," I yelled back at her, grinning, and envying her her effortless courage.

I looked down at my shopping cart. It contained Jeannie's and my mother's contributions plus six packages of spaghetti I had run into Almacs to buy, fearful that I might forget my promise to Jeannie. I looked at Charlayne. It was time to make small talk, but my mind had suddenly gone blank. Charlayne's cart had hardly anything in it. There were a few cans, some paper napkins, and some Kleenex.

"How long you been here?" I asked stupidly. Even though half my body was hidden behind the sign, I felt naked without Bernie. I pushed some more words out. "Did you come straight from school?"

"Um. Hmmm. Can't tell from the cart but I've been here the better part of an hour." Charlayne had that soft, syrupy, southern way of talking that sounds like someone humming a lullaby. "Not much action. But I bet people will feel a little more like donating things now that you and Bernie are here."

For a moment I didn't know what she was talking about, but then I realized and felt embarrassed and strangely guilty. I stuck my hands in my pockets and tried to hunch down behind the sign. I wished my skin would turn brown so that I wouldn't feel so different.

Charlayne just smiled and looked straight at me with two dark eyes.

"Doesn't this stuff scare you?" I asked so quietly I was afraid she might not hear me. "I mean, you were awfully brave doing this by yourself. Me, I'm scared to death and I'm not even . . ." I faded off, shocked by what I had almost said. My face was burning red and I realized that I had gotten my wish—I certainly wasn't white anymore.

"Negro?" Charlayne just laughed. "The truth is, my friend Ruthie was supposed to come today but at the last moment she chickened out. You're not the only one who gets scared, you know. I've just got more experience than you."

"Yeah, I guess not," I said gratefully. Here I was acting like a complete idiot and she was trying to put me at ease.

"I was scared once. Back in Georgia. We did a sit-in last year at a lunch counter. To integrate it. We all sat down in the white section and ordered ice-cream sodas—vanilla," she laughed. "But it was too much for the lady behind the counter. She started to cry and pulled her apron up over her face. Then she got the manager. And *he* got the cops, and you better believe I was scared."

"What happened then?" I asked. I could hardly believe it. Charlayne was a real, live freedom fighter.

"Well, we all went limp and they carried us away."

"You went limp? Why?"

"To keep from getting hurt. Passive resistance. Nonviolence. You go limp so it's hard to drag you but they don't have an excuse to beat you up. It's what Reverend King preaches. We all had to take a course in it before we could participate in the sit-in."

"Where did they take you?"

"To the police station. They put us in a room called the 'concentration room.' They said if we knew what was good for us we'd better 'con-cen-trate' on what we had done. So you know what we did?"

"What?"

"Sang every freedom song we knew as loud as we could sing them."

"And then what?"

"They arrested the older kids and the rest of us felt cheated."

"You mean you *wanted* to go to jail?"

"In a way. Not really, though. I mean, those kids have police records now."

"Are they still there? The older kids?"

"No," Charlayne laughed. "We had a bail fund and a good lawyer."

"A lawyer?"

"A young white guy who works for the NAACP. It took a while, but in a few days they were all out, hoarse from singing and ready to try all over again. . . . When I graduate, I'm going back down south to work for civil rights. Even then, I'll bet there will still be things to do."

"Wow!" I said. "Wow!"

"Wow, what?" Bernie asked. She was loading several cans of tuna into her cart and eyeing Charlayne and me suspiciously. "You guys gonna stand around and talk all day or you gonna do any work? Betsy, don't you think it's about time you *did* something?" She tilted her head toward a young woman who was coming out of the supermarket. "This is it, Bets, go to it!"

I nodded, took a deep breath, thought about Charlayne at the lunch counter and walked over toward the woman. Her shopping cart was filled to the brim with groceries, meat, vegetables, a couple of melons, and, sitting in the center of it all, a round, ripe, year-old baby who looked like he might have just been checked out at the meat counter along with a turkey.

"Ah-hem." I cleared my throat. The woman didn't seem to hear me. "Ah—ah—excuse me," I added.

"Zoom. Zoom," the baby said, gurgling and pointing at me.

"No, Petie," the woman said to him. "That's not a zoom-zoom. It's a girl. I don't know *why*, but he thinks you're a truck. I guess it's the sign. Okay, let's see it," she said, standing back to read. "Down south? Well, that's certainly a worthy cause. How about some canned fruit?" She reached into the pile, drew out some pears and peaches, and handed them to me. "That should do it. Thanks."

"Right," I said. "You're welcome." Somehow I didn't feel like a freedom fighter or a hero. I still felt like a northern fried chicken. I'd managed to do absolutely nothing and get away with it. But as I brought the two cans back to the cart, I could feel my nervousness slowly melting away. This was a whole lot easier than I'd thought. People were really nice. Charlayne and Bernie were each off with other people, so I went after a heavy blond woman who was loading groceries into the trunk of her car.

"We're collecting food," I said. "To send down south. To help Negro people get their civil rights. Would you like to donate something?"

"Pardon?" The woman pulled her head out of her trunk and stared at me, puzzled.

"I said that we're—uh—collecting food to send down south to—uh—help people get their civil rights. Would you—"

"Oh, sure. Just a sec." She was back in the trunk."Here. It isn't much, but maybe it will help." She handed me some canned string beans and large jar of cooked chicken.

"Thanks," I said. I felt wonderful."Look!" I shouted to Bernie. I waved the can of string beans in the air like it was a victory flag.

"Not bad for a beginner," Bernie said, grinning. She was balancing a bottle of ketchup on top of a box of Quaker Oats and a can of Hawaiian Punch.

In front of me was a young woman with long, stringy, no-color hair. She wheeled a cart loaded with everything from cat food to a large boxed chocolate cake.

"Hi!" I said, feeling confident. "I'm collecting food to send down south to help Negro people with their civil rights. Would you—"

"Too busy," she said, continuing on her way.

I figured she had misunderstood. "Oh, that's okay," I said. "You don't have to do any work—just donate some food."

"Young lady," she snapped, stopping to let go of her cart, "do your parents know what you're doing here?"

"I—uh—yes, yes, they do."

"Well, *this* is the limit!"

For a few seconds we stood completely still just staring at one another. A beauty mark, like a tiny raisin, vibrated ever so slightly on the woman's cheek, just below her left eye.

"Look, you're young," she finally said. She took a deep breath and looked sadly at me. "Perhaps you don't realize. If the Lord had meant us to be one and the same, he would have painted us all the same color. Believe me, the colored people were put on earth for a separate purpose—"

"Yes, ma'am," a heavy-accented voice intruded, "to serve dee white folk."

From out of nowhere, Charlayne suddenly appeared and did a weird kind of a step—something like an old soft shoe—shuffling her feet on the pavement and nodding and bowing her head. She grabbed the woman's cart and started pushing it.

"Which way to dee auto-*mo*bile, missus?"

"It's the—uh—blue Chevy over there. But really, you don't have to—"

"No, no, ma'am. It a pleas-juh to serve you," Charlayne said, grinning and bowing and casting a quick smile my way.

The woman had no choice but to follow, and I reluctantly trailed a couple of feet behind, not sure whether the performance I was witnessing was a comedy or a tragedy and whether I was enjoying it or not. When we got to the car, Charlayne loaded the groceries—four heavy bags—into the rear seat of the woman's car. I stood and watched from a distance as the woman withdrew a folded dollar bill from her purse to give to Charlayne.

For a split second Charlayne's face grew red and angry, but then she seemed to shake herself. A second later she was smiling and I wasn't even sure I had seen what I had seen.

"Thanks, that's very kind of you," Charlayne said in her normal speaking voice, "but it really isn't necessary."

The woman was truly flustered. "But I—won't you accept . ."

"You could donate some food to our cause, if you'd like. We're sending things down south to people who haven't anything much to eat."

Without a word, the woman reached into one of the bags and handed Charlayne a bottle of cranberry juice and a huge box of rice. It wasn't clear to me whether she had changed her mind about "the colored people" or whether she believed she was being held up by a thief and her accomplice.

"That's awfully generous," Charlayne said, smiling a clear, direct, nonaccusing smile. "Thank you."

"Yeah," I added unnecessarily.

"You're welcome." The woman climbed nervously into her car.

"Thanks for rescuing me," I said to Charlayne as we walked back to the shopping carts. "You really are amazing, you know!"

"Yes." Charlayne's laugh was lilting. "I confess. Sometimes I even amaze myself. Twice I wanted to haul off and belt her—first when she was lacing into you, and then when she wanted to pay me like I was her servant or something. But in the end—well—some people take a long time to learn."

"You know, you're even braver than Bernie. I wish she could have seen you in operation. She'd have loved it." I looked around the parking lot for her. "Where *is* she?"

"Over there," Charlayne said, pointing.

At the other end of the parking lot, Bernie was leaning seductively against a tan Volkswagen beetle with a Brown University sticker on the back, talking to the handsomest guy I'd ever seen.

"Leave it to Bernie," I mumbled.

"What?" Charlayne asked.

"Nothing," I said, feeling annoyed with Bernie for the second time that day.

Charlayne and I went back to work. I felt great. For once I was *doing* something, not just thinking about it, and the best part was that I wasn't scared anymore. Not even of the one or two people who refused to donate anything. I wanted to tell Bernie; I knew she'd be proud of me. But Bernie was still talking to the boy from Brown. Charlayne's and my baskets were nearly full, but Bernie's stood half-empty.

It was almost quarter to six. At six o'clock, someone was coming from PROJECT to pick up our groceries and deliver them to the distribution center at the Benefit Street Church. Charlayne was off giving her speech to an old woman and I decided it was time to wrench Bernie away from her new "man."

I walked over to the Volkswagen. Bernie was leaning against the car, her head tilted up toward the boy like he was the sun and she was trying to get a tan.

"Bernie," I called.

She pivoted slowly and elegantly toward me. "Oh," she said in her Jacqueline Kennedy voice. "It's Elizabeth! Biff, this is my very best friend, Elizabeth Bergman. Elizabeth—Biff Manly."

"Manly?" I repeated in disbelief.

"Man l-e-y," Biff spelled out.

"I'm Betsy. Just plain Betsy. Only Ber-*niece*," I said, eyeing Bernie, "calls me Elizabeth. So, what's the story, Ber-*niece?* You guys gonna stand around and talk all day or you gonna do any work?"

Bernie looked embarrassed, and Biff quickly became absorbed in checking the air in his tires. "Gee, Bets, I hope you won't mind, but Biff asked me to go for a ride with him. He's going to show me the campus."

"Bernie, you've seen the Brown campus a hundred times." Bernie gave me a look that could have withered the Wicked Witch of the West. "Oh, sure," I said, catching on. "Fine, but how am I supposed to get home? Drive your parents' car? You know how they'd feel about that. And besides, Bernie"—I tried to lower my voice, but despite my good intentions, it boomed—"BIFF MANLEY! Ira Schwartz, David Hertzberg, Irving Spiegel maybe, but *BIFF* MANLEY—you want to send your parents to an early death?"

Manley stood up, opened the door to his car, and started examining the interior of his glove compartment as if there were a movie inside.

Bernie led me forceably by the arm from the car. "Kindly *lower your voice!*" she commanded. "I'm sorry, Betsy. I know you're right, but look at him. He's sensational. He's an absolute hunk!"

I felt sick to my stomach.

"Biff's gonna bring me back in an hour or so and I'll drive the car back. I'll tell my parents that things ran late here. You can take the bus . . . or"—she looked suspiciously at Charlayne—"you can get a ride with your new friend."

"That's a good idea," I said, furious. "Maybe I will. After all, it's good to have friends you can rely on. So don't even give me another thought. Just enjoy yourself with *Barf.* I'll be seeing you." I turned away and didn't look back. Even so, I could feel Bernie's eyes on me. I hoped she felt rotten.

When I turned around again to steal a glance at Bernie, it was from the safety of my shopping cart. I had nothing to fear, though, because Barf Manley was already backing out of his parking spot with Bernie next to him, too absorbed in her conquest to notice anything but him.

"Betsy!" a familiar voice shouted. "Charlie!" the voice called to Charlayne, who was thrashing about not far from me, trying to pull her sign off over her head.

I looked up and there, standing in the rear of an old blue pickup truck, was Janet Bloom.

"Hello!" she yelled. "You guys have done a great job." She jumped down from the truck and walked over to our carts. "Where's Bernie?"

"She—had to leave early—unexpectedly." I realized that I was addressing my remarks mainly to the pavement. I couldn't bear to raise my eyes and look directly at either Charlayne or Janet. I'm not very good at lying.

"Yes," Charlayne jumped in confidently, "you know how it is. These things happen now and again—the unexpected."

I glanced quickly and gratefully at Charlayne while Janet looked back and forth at us, clearly puzzled. "Well, I hope everything's okay. My mom's waiting in the truck. If either of you needs a ride home, you're welcome to come along with us if you don't mind stopping first to deliver this stuff to the distribution center."

"That'd be great," I said.

"Yes, thanks," Charlayne said.

"Aren't you going to introduce me to your friends?" Janet's mother jumped down from the cab of the pickup truck.

"Oh, sure. Betsy Bergman, Charlie Perry—my mom."

"Hi," I said awkwardly. I wasn't used to seeing my friends' mothers leap out of trucks, and on top of that I remembered that Janet's mother was a lawyer. What did you call a woman lawyer? I'd never met one before. Sir? Madam? Counselor?

"Frieda," she said, reaching out her hand to give mine and Charlayne's a shake. "But if you want to get on my good side, you'll call me Fred."

Silently I decided to do my best to avoid calling her anything. In a pinch, it would be Mrs. Bloom. Frieda just wasn't motherly.

Janet wheeled my cart over to the pickup truck and I went for Bernie's cart while Charlayne pushed her own. With Mrs. Bloom's help, we loaded the truck. Janet and her mother had made an earlier stop at another supermarket and the back of the truck already contained several cartons of food.

"Any trouble?" Mrs. Bloom asked us.

"Oh, Fred." Janet sounded slightly annoyed. "You're always ready for action. Does it look to you like they had any trouble? . . . The long arm of the law," she said nodding her head in her mother's direction, "at a moment's notice, ready to reach for the gavel and swing into action."

I opened my mouth to tell Mrs. Bloom about the woman who had asked if my parents knew what I was doing, but then I closed it again. That really wasn't trouble, I thought. Just life.

"Nope, no trouble," Charlayne was saying. "But then, I didn't tell them how I was planning to move into their neighborhood."

Janet, her mother, and Charlayne laughed and I laughed, too, even though I wasn't exactly sure I'd gotten the joke.

Janet and her mother climbed into the cab of the pickup truck and Charlayne and I loaded ourselves into the back. Sitting on a carton, we had a great view of the world as Mrs. Bloom pulled out of the parking lot and drove us down Angell Street.

This was the "East Side"—the old, elegant, graceful part of Providence, high on a hill where beautiful mansions stood, dating from the early days when a few wealthy families dominated the city. We bumped and rattled down the long street past the red walls of the Brown campus—made redder by the autumn-colored ivy—past Bernie, who I imagined was sitting with Biff under some ancient campus elm, and on down the great hill toward Benefit Street. It was close to twilight and the city was slowing down—putting on soft slippers, like a sleepy old man at the end of the day.

We turned left onto Benefit Street past the Rhode Island School of Design Museum and headed toward the thin gray spire of the Benefit Street Church. People with black skin turned to bronze by the fading sunlight and white skin turned to amber were loading a van with Mississippi plates. Under his breath, a man was humming a tune I didn't recognize. Except for the occasional clink of jars and the rattle of paper, there was very little sound. Everyone seemed joined together in a long human chain by a kind of silent rhythm. One person lifted a carton of food from a car and swung it to another, who swung it to a third, and on down the line until it was finally loaded onto the van by a young Negro man and woman.

Without a word, I climbed out of the van and Charlayne lowered a carton over the side to me. When I turned around to find a way to join the human chain, a Negro boy had suddenly appeared out of nowhere. He swung his long arms out to me to take the carton and smiled as he passed the box on to a thin old white woman of about seventy. Janet's mother had climbed into the back of the pickup truck and, with Charlayne, was lowering boxes over the side. Two cartons descended toward me at once, but when I reached up, straining impossibly to catch them both, Janet was suddenly at my side, catching one and smiling.

We worked together—hauling and lifting, swinging our arms, part of that strange, silent rhythm, and somehow I felt so close to everyone, as if Janet and Charlayne and Frieda and I were all sisters and all the strange people—black and white—were relatives.

Too soon, the pickup truck was empty and it was time to go. Janet and Frieda shook hands with a Negro man who was wearing a clerical collar. He looked up at Charlayne and me in the back of the truck and touched his hand to the center of his forehead and then waved it out toward us in a kind of salute. But before I could wave back, he had turned and disappeared into the growing shadows.

Janet hopped in the back with us and her mother drove us slowly away from the church, back again down Benefit Street all the way to the end of it, past Cady, Howland, Church, and Star Streets—all the tiny, steep, mysterious streets that slipped down the hill and into the twinkling city.

In the back of the truck, the cool breeze turned to cold wind and we huddled together to keep warm, our backbones banging first against each other and then against the hard metal walls of the van. Janet's mother turned right on Olney Street, left on Camp, and then right again into some old, run-down streets I had been near but never in.

Charlayne leaned over to knock on the glass window of the cab to tell Mrs. Bloom it was time to stop. The truck slowed to a halt and Charlayne stretched her right leg out straight, moving it up and down with her hands to get some feeling back in it. She pointed to a two-family house that was small and in need of a coat of paint. "That's mine," she said.

Outside it, a little girl with hair in a dozen tiny little braids bounced up and down, up and down on her toes. "Charlie!" she called when she saw that it was Charlayne.

"Hello, pie face," Charlayne yelled back. "My sister, Pauline," she said to us. "Always moving." Charlayne climbed out of the truck and walked around to the front to speak to Mrs. Bloom. "Thanks for the ride." She waved to Janet and me. "Thanks, Janet. *Hasta la vista*, Betsy. See you in Spanish."

"Yeah," I said "*Adiós. Hasta la próxima vez.* See you in Spanish." I wrinkled up my nose in mock disgust, but it was really to hide the strange, sad feeling I had inside. I didn't understand it. It was as if by leaving, I was afraid of losing Charlayne.

"Bye, Charlie," Janet yelled, and we drove farther up the long hill to Hope Street and headed for Pawtucket, Janet and I pressed flat against the walls of the truck like piecrust in a pan.

When we turned up Mayflower Avenue, the streetlamps were already on and the windows in the houses glowed with soft yellow light. I could smell steak and onions frying in Mrs. Chirch's kitchen. Taking my cue from Charlayne, I rapped on the window of the cab to tell Mrs. Bloom where to stop.

Janet and I jumped down from the back, Janet to get into the cab where it was warm, and I to say goodbye to her mother. "Thanks for the ride, Mrs. Bloom."

"Frieda," she said.

"Frieda," I agreed.

"Next time, Fred," she added.

"Aw, mom," Janet moaned. "You overdo it sometimes."

"Maybe so, but nevertheless, next time, Fred."

"Okay," I said. I liked her. She was tough.

Janet was standing beside me. "Thanks for the help, Betsy." She smiled at me and, despite how cold I was, suddenly I felt warm and terribly, terribly shy.

"Thank *you,*" I said, not moving.

"See you," Janet said.

"Yeah," I said. "See you." The two of us just stood there gazing awkwardly at each other.

"Well, bye," Janet said again, finally getting into the cab.

"Yeah, bye," I said, but I didn't budge and I didn't turn to go inside until the pickup truck reached the top of Mayflower Avenue, turned, and was completely out of sight.

7

Three weeks later, on a stormy afternoon in late October, Bernie and I lay flat on our stomachs on the scratchy carpet of my den holding hands. Fat, round raindrops crackled and snapped like popcorn against the glass windowpanes and the wind blew smoke-gray clouds across the sky.

The old Zenith radio that had belonged to my grandmother blasted Chubby Checker's voice singing "The Twist," but we barely moved. We waited, instead, by the radio, listening for news of the end of the world.

As we waited, U.S. Navy ships surrounded Cuba, anticipating the approach of twenty-five Russian ships. A few days before, President Kennedy had announced that the Soviet Union was secretly shipping nuclear missiles to Cuba, missiles that could be used to attack the United States. He had ordered a naval blockade, and now the whole world was holding its breath.

I rolled onto my side and sat up. "What do you think's going to happen, Bernie? Will there be nuclear war?"

"Who knows?" Bernie answered. For once she seemed frightened. "Anything could happen. The Americans could attack the Russian ships, or, worse, maybe someone in Moscow or Washington will do something stupid. . . ."

"You mean, like push the button?"

Bernie nodded.

"But Bernie, the whole world could blow up!"

"Worse still," Bernie said. "We could all die of radiation sickness."

"Bernie," I whispered, "be quiet!"

"I'm sorry," she said. "Really sorry."

"Well, you don't have to be so upset. I only meant that you were scaring me to—"

"No—that's not what I mean. I'm sorry for the day at Almacs."

"Don't worry about it," I said quickly, wondering why she was bringing it up now. "It was nothing. I hardly remember it."

Bernie stared suspiciously at me. She knew I was lying. I'd thought often about that day, but I hadn't had the nerve to discuss it. There was something about it that bothered me. It was more than just being angry with Bernie. It was something different about me. And though I knew I was chickening out, I couldn't help it. I had the strongest feeling that talking about whatever was disturbing me would only make things worse between Bernie and me. Instead of clearing things up, it would open up some new, uncharted area. It was better to let it all pass.

"Whatever happened to manly Barf Manley?" I asked, steering the conversation into safer waters.

"He wanted to sneak me up to his dorm," Bernie said, lowering her eyes. "When I refused, that was the end of it." She paused for a moment. "But you knew he was a dud right from the start, didn't you? Just from looking at him."

"Not really. I just didn't think you should go off with someone you didn't know—I don't think you should be a 'pick-up.' "

"You're right, Betsy. When it comes to men, I get carried away."

"I know," I said. There was a lot more I had to say, but again I couldn't bring myself to say it. Instead, I got up and switched the dial searching for news. President Kennedy's voice filled the room.

> . . . it shall be the policy of the nation to regard any nuclear missile launched from Cuba against any nation in the Western Hemisphere as an attack by the Soviet Union on the United States requiring full retaliatory response on the Soviet Union. . . .

"That's old stuff," Bernie whispered, reassuring me. "It's what he said Monday night on TV. Nothing's happened yet. The Russian ships must still be approaching."

Then the radio announcer confirmed Bernie's theory.

"Why now?" I asked.

"Why now what?" Bernie said.

"Why are you apologizing all of a sudden?"

"Oh, I don't know." Bernie looked a little bit embarrassed. "It's just that if the world's going to end, I want to set things straight between us. I don't want you to be angry."

"It's okay. I *was* angry, but I'm not now."

Bernie's grateful smile made me feel strangely powerful. *"Ayudeme* with my Spanish," I said, reaching for my Spanish book and trying again to change the subject.

"I will, if you'll help me with my Hebrew." Bernie frowned. She had just started taking conversational Hebrew at the temple.

"Right," I said. *"Gesundheit."*

"That's not Hebrew, dummy."

"Well, what did you expect from me?"

Bernie gave me a shove and then hunkered down over her Hebrew book, trying to concentrate.

The radio was playing music again—another twist. Through the archway I could see Jeannie in the living room. She stood in front of the fireplace stuffing her mouth with spaghetti and tomato sauce from a plate she had balanced on the mantelpiece. In between each dripping mouthful, she moved in time to the music—knees bent and legs twisting open and closed, open and closed. Her face and blouse were speckled with tomato sauce. She looked like she had broken out in poison ivy.

"Yuk!" I yelled involuntarily. The conversation with Bernie, the business of nuclear war, was bad enough. I felt tense, and Jeannie's presence made me even more so. Bernie looked up and Jeannie turned to face me, a strand of red spaghetti dripping from the side of her mouth like blood.

"What's the matter?" she asked.

"Nothing. Except why do you have to dance and eat at the same time? Why can't you do one thing at a time like everyone else? And why do you have to be in the living room? You have spaghetti sauce on the mirror."

Jeannie's face clouded over. "I wanted to be close to the radio—close to you. There isn't much time left, you know."

"Excuse me?"

"There isn't much time left," Jeannie repeated, her eyes filling with tears.

"For what?"

"For eating spaghetti or dancing or anything!" Jeannie shouted angrily. Then she burst into tears and ran wailing from the room.

"What did I do now?" I asked God, shrugging and looking skyward.

"You hurt her," Bernie answered somewhat angrily. "*You're* afraid to die. She is, *too*. You ought to go easier on her."

"You're right," I said. I felt low and disgusting. Like the night crawlers I'd seen pictured on the bait-shop signs out by Narragansett Pier.

"Jeannie," I called, getting to my feet and walking to the foot of the hall stairs. "Jeannie?" I yelled. "Please."

Upstairs a door slammed and I knew I had done it again. Behind me, something rattled. My mother opened the door, her keys in her hand. Dressed in a charcoal-gray suit that was dripping wet, she was returning from the stockbrokers, where she went twice a week now to watch the ticker tape and decide which stocks to buy and sell.

"What's happening?" she asked immediately.

"Nothing," I answered guiltily. "Jeannie and I just had a—"

"The news. The news," she repeated in a tight, unfamiliar voice.

"Oh," I said, "nothing yet. The ships are still approaching. And the navy is still waiting. . . . How's the stock-market business?"

"Okay," she answered, but she looked strained as she followed me into the den. "The market's down, of course. Everything's mixed up today. Hello, Bernie."

"Hi, Mrs. Bergman. How's it going?"

"Okay, I guess," she sighed. Then she cleared her throat and looked at me. "I've decided to quit this stock-market thing, Betsy. I know I said I wouldn't, but it just isn't working out."

"But why?" I tried to keep my voice level. I was determined not to let her see my anger and frustration. I was determined not to explode. I had done enough damage for one day. "What's not to work out? You're not *employed* there. You just sit . . ."

Bernie's eyes narrowed and she shot me a warning glance.

" . . . and watch and learn things," I added quickly, trying to put a smile on my face at the end of the sentence.

"But I'm uncomfortable," she said. "I'm the only woman. It's all men."

"So what?" I asked, too loudly. "I mean," I said, adjusting my tone to a low, casual one, "what difference does that make?"

"It makes me uncomfortable, that's all. I'm starting to feel like . . ." She trailed off.

"Like what?"

"Well, like their—pet. You know, cute and underfoot."

Bernie laughed. But she didn't know about my mother's problem. My mother smiled at her.

"I'll do it from home now, instead of going in person. I'll call up and get the quotes over the phone."

"What's the difference between that and what you always did?"

"Nothing much, I guess, but . . ." She raised one hand sadly in the air and let it drop to her lap. "I can't help it. I know this kind of thing annoys and disappoints you. . . . I'm joining a book-discussion group. I know that will work out. It starts Tuesday."

"Great," I said without enthusiasm. "Maybe you—"

"We interrupt this program to bring you a bulletin. A ship reportedly under charter to the Soviet Union is approaching the United States naval blockade. Further information as soon as it is available. Repeat. A ship reportedly under charter . . ."

No one breathed.

"Where's Jeannie?" I said, running out of the room. "I have to apologize."

Bernie stayed overnight in my bed and so did Jeannie. It was pretty crowded, but it didn't matter. The three of us hardly slept. We hugged each other and stayed up all night listening to the radio. At about seven the next morning while we were getting dressed for school, some men from the *Joseph P. Kennedy, Jr.,* a naval destroyer, boarded the chartered ship to search it for weapons. The ship passed inspection and was allowed to pass through the blockade.

Later that day as we sat red-eyed through our classes, the principal announced over the public-address system that many Soviet ships had turned back and that the ones that had not were carrying oil, not weapons. President Kennedy, he said, was a hero. He had saved the world.

"The meeting will now come to order," Neil Segal said. He stood behind the long table at the front of the room and banged a hammer on a small block of wood. It was the first PROJECT meeting of the year. "Any old business?" he asked.

"Oh, Betsy, isn't he cute?" Bernie mumbled. She made a fork out of her middle three fingers, inserted it into the center of her hair, and lifted her bouffant higher.

I didn't answer. "Cute" was a word I reserved for tiny babies and for monkeys at the zoo. Besides, I was too busy watching Kenny Klein, who was sitting just to Neil Segal's right. He seemed to be looking straight at me. I shifted uncomfortably in my seat, thinking how silly I was to think he was staring at me and how he was really only staring blankly at the group.

A few rows ahead of us, Sally Axelrod raised her hand.

"Yes?" Neil said.

"I just wanted to inform the membership that over the summer we appointed Bernie Levin to the Nominating Committee."

There was some polite applause as Bernie straightened her back and smiled graciously at everyone like a famous film star.

While Penny Prince—or, as Bernie calls her, "La Princesse"—reported some boring stuff about the Refreshment

Committee's budget problems, Kenny wrote something on a slip of yellow paper. He passed it to Janet Bloom, who, as secretary, sat next to him furiously scribbling on a stenographer's pad, taking down everything that was being said. Glancing quickly at the yellow paper, she nodded and went on with her notes, never missing a beat. I wished I could trade places with her and sit next to Kenny.

"Any more old business?" Neil asked. He gazed up and down the rows of chairs.

"Don't you just love the way he handles things?" Bernie whispered. "He's incredible!" She sighed deeply.

"Oh, Bernie," I groaned. I reached my arm high in the air to stretch a kink out of it.

"The chair acknowledges Betsy Bergman," Neil said.

"Oh," I gasped, feeling all the color drain from my face. I had never *ever* spoken at a PROJECT meeting—it was way too scary—and now I'd have to explain that I hadn't really meant to raise my hand. I scrambled to my feet. "I was only trying to . . ." I couldn't go on. Kenny Klein was definitely staring at me now. For once I had his complete attention. Say something, say something, I kept telling myself. I looked down at Bernie for help. She moved her shoulders up and down in an almost imperceptible shrug. "I was only trying to—to tell you that— that, um—" My eyes clouded over and I had difficulty seeing. What's more, I could barely breathe. "—that I. . . ." I trailed off, too humiliated to continue. "I'm sorry—I can't—"

"Didn't you want to report on the Food for Freedom drive?" Janet called out. She had stopped taking notes to come to my rescue. She smiled, and I was filled with the same warm feeling I had experienced that cold, magical night in the truck.

"Yes, sure," I said, swallowing. "Thanks. I was trying to tell you that, um, on October first, Janet—that is, Janet Bloom— and Bernie Levin and I and another girl, Charlayne Perry, from the Baptist Youth Fellowship, collected several cartons of food from Almacs Supermarket and delivered them to the distribution center at the Benefit Street Church." I stopped. I was out of breath and out of words. "Well, that's it," I said. "That was what

I wanted to say." I looked miserably at Neil Segal and from the corner of my eye stole a glance at Kenny Klein. He was still staring at me, but it was impossible to tell what he was thinking.

"Thanks, Betsy," Neil said. He took his hammer in his hand and was about to slam it down again on the wood block when Janet interrupted.

"I'd like to add something."

Neil nodded to her.

"What Betsy doesn't know is that Carol Schwartz and Stanley Katz"—she nodded to two kids in the back—"also collected food at Stop and Shop. And with the help of church groups at supermarkets throughout the city, we sent two truckloads of food down south."

I nodded to Janet and collapsed like a broken umbrella into my chair while everyone applauded.

"You shouldn't have said that I helped," Bernie whispered, looking apologetic. "You know I didn't do much that day."

"It's okay. Don't worry about it," I said quickly. "Just do me a favor. Don't talk to me now. I have to catch my breath." My body was trembling.

Bernie touched my arm. "Easy, Bets."

I nodded. It was all I could do. I still couldn't speak and I was fairly certain that I was about to die of a heart attack.

They went on to new business and Janet was speaking again, saying something about a housing project. ". . . so they're planning a demonstration sometime in February and they're hoping as many of us as possible will participate. I'm passing around a sheet of paper. If you think you'll be able to come, sign your name so we'll have a vague idea of the numbers. I'll let you know as soon as I do about the date, time, et cetera."

"What did she say?" I mumbled out of the side of my mouth, turning my head ever so slightly and keeping my hands folded tightly in my lap. I didn't dare move for fear that someone would call on me again.

"Oh, something about that integrated housing project they want to build on the hill. You know, the one everybody's making such a fuss about. In her spare time, your dear friend Janet Bloom is helping to organize a demonstration to support it."

I turned carefully toward Bernie and unfolded my hands. I had clasped them so tightly they were turning white. "How come you dislike her so much? I got to know her at the Food for Freedom thing. She's nice," I said, feeling suddenly shy and embarrassed.

"She gets on my nerves. She's way too serious. She's almost inhuman." Bernie passed me a clipboard with a sheet of paper attached to it. It was the list of names for the demonstration. Already there were about ten signatures, but Bernie hadn't added hers yet.

"Aren't you going to sign it?" I asked.

"You know me," she said, eyeing Neil Segal, who was speaking again. "I can't commit myself that far in advance. You can never tell what might turn up."

"Right," I said, thinking angrily that if Janet Bloom was way too serious, what was Bernie?

The clipboard lay in my lap. Stuck behind the clip on a piece of string was a nibbled yellow pencil. I fingered the pencil and then noticed a small piece of yellow paper stuck underneath the list. In tiny letters in red ink, Janet had written her name. Not just her name, though. A whole series of names. In the form of a question. "Janet. Janet who? Janet Bloom? Janet Bloom. And who's that? We'll know soon." I smiled. I wondered what it meant and whether she knew she had written a poem. She didn't sound inhuman to me.

I stuck the poem back under the list and turned the clipboard right side up, staring again at the list of names. If only Bernie would sign it, then I would have the courage to add my name. I glanced at her. She was listening attentively to Neil Segal, who was talking about membership. I didn't think she was particularly interested in the number of new members PROJECT had acquired this year but rather in the way his lips formed each word.

A demonstration, I thought. That was something much bigger and scarier than collecting food to send down south. That was visible, using your body to make a statement about what you believed. I picked up the pencil to sign my name. "Be careful, Betsy. You never know. . . ." My mother's warning voice whistled through my head. I put the pencil back behind the clip and stared again at the list of names. The board felt heavy in my lap.

Behind me, someone tapped my shoulder. I turned around. It was funny-faced Mickey Epstein. With tiny dark eyes and tan skin, he looked like a chocolate chip cookie.

"You finished, yet?" he asked.

"Oh, yeah, sure," I said, flustered. I passed him the clipboard, relieved that now I didn't have time to sign my name.

The thick, inviting smell of coffee floated toward me, and the meeting broke for refreshments. In the back of the social hall, Penny Prince stood by two large urns pouring cups of coffee and tea. The way she did it—chin high, neck and back perfectly straight, lips pursed—I knew that in her eyes the kitchen urn was an antique silver samovar, the paper cups delicate bone china, and serving us merely an unpleasant job that would soon be over.

Bernie disappeared into the crowd, headed in Neil Segal's direction, but I had my eye on a platter of tiny Danish pastries at La Princesse's elbow.

"Coffee or tea?" La Princesse asked crisply, looking just slightly to the left of my face. I turned around to see whom she was speaking to and realized it was me.

"Tea, please, and two lumps." That was probably the longest sentence I'd said to her in my entire life. I reached for a napkin and a sticky brown pastry.

"Hi, Betsy!" Janet stood flushed and excited before me. There was something about the way she had suddenly appeared that made me think of a race car that had just wheeled victoriously into the finish line. "How are you?"

"Fine," I answered, realizing with amazement that all the pleasure on her face was the result of seeing me. "Thanks for saving me today. I was scared to death," I said, staring into her smiling eyes. "Neil thought I was raising my hand, but I was really only stretching."

"I know," Janet whispered. "Don't worry about it. You were fine."

"With some help from my friends," I said, blushing on the word "friends." It seemed a little premature, but Janet didn't seem to mind or notice.

"I haven't looked at my clipboard yet. Did you sign up for the demonstration?"

"No," I said slowly. I was about to lie—mumble something lame about not knowing what my plans would be—when, for a reason I couldn't figure, I decided instead to tell the truth. "I just couldn't do it. I'm sorry. There are some things I just can't do. . . . A demonstration—well, it's too much. . . . Do you know what I mean?"

"I guess so." Janet's face showed disappointment. "Well, maybe you'll change your mind."

"She won't. Her mind's made up," an angry voice interrupted.

I jumped. It was Bernie. She'd apparently been listening in on my conversation. She added her two cents and then quickly disappeared into the crowd.

"I don't think she likes me," Janet said.

"Don't pay attention." I leaned over and whispered a little shyly in Janet's ear. "I think she's jealous that we're getting to be—that we're friendly."

Janet smiled shyly but didn't say anything.

Together we walked over to where everyone was clustered awaiting the start of the friendship circle. Janet started talking to Sally Axelrod, something about the next meeting, but I just nodded and smiled, only pretending to listen to what they were saying. Instead, I watched Bernie across the room.

From the way she stood, posed like a fashion model in an elongated, artificial stance, it was obvious to me and probably to anyone else who was interested that she was flirting with Neil Segal. He was laughing at something Bernie was saying. I wished I could be invisible and listen in. I was envious. I wished small talk and sweet nothings came easier to me. It seemed to be the ingredient of most conversations.

Near Bernie and Neil, sexy Sybil Kaye stood weaving her magic web around Kenny Klein. She pouted, arched her back, and pointed her breasts out toward Kenny in an exaggerated way. As they talked, I noticed that he seemed to be addressing his remarks to her chest instead of to her face. I wondered whether Sybil Kaye knew, and, if she did, whether she cared.

Kenny excused himself and reached for a glass from the table behind him. He walked to the center of the room and banged the glass several times with a spoon. The glass made a tinkling, musical sound, and slowly the mumbling that filled the room diminished. "Friendship circle," Kenny called out, and then walked over to a table near me to deposit the glass. The mumbling began again as everyone dispensed with the remains of their refreshments and formed a huge ring around the room.

"Hi, Betsy and Ber—whoops, sorry. Force of habit, I guess." Suddenly Kenny Klein was beside me. "I'm so used to seeing you and Bernie together."

"I know," I said, measuring out my words. I hoped that if I was slow and careful, I wouldn't sound nervous and idiotic.

"Hope Neil didn't unnerve you too much today. You were just stretching, weren't you?" he laughed.

"Yes! How did *you* know? Janet told you, didn't she?"

"Nope," he said. "I was watching you. That red sweater."

I looked down at my sweater. "What about it?"

"You look nice in it."

"I do?" I asked stupidly.

Kenny just nodded. He took my right hand in his left hand and suddenly I knew exactly how it felt to float gently upward in a hot-air balloon. Warm and light and slightly tingly. Like a bubble rising in a glass of ginger ale. It doesn't mean anything, I thought, trying to let a little of the air out of the balloon. It's only a friendship circle. Janet was on my other side and I concentrated on taking her hand.

Everyone crossed right hand over left. Soon we were all linked in a chain that extended in a circle around the room. Across the way, Bernie winked slyly at me, her left hand in Neil Segal's right. Someone started singing *"Henay ma tov uma nayim"* and we all joined in, slowly swaying back and forth in time to the melody. *"Henay ma tov uma nayim shevet achim gam yachud. Henay ma tov uma nayim shevet achim gam yachud."* How good and lovely it is for people to dwell together on the earth in harmony. Over and over again we sang the Hebrew words in a slow, rhythmic, chantlike beat that increased ever so slightly in speed each time we repeated the verse. Janet and a few others sang in harmony and, using her voice as guide, so did I. Everything—the music, the unbroken chain of friends; my body swaying slowly in rhythm touching Kenny's shoulder on one side, Janet's on the other—made the balloon soar higher and higher into the sky, bobbing in and out of layers of soft white clouds, floating, floating, floating right up to the sun.

The late-afternoon sun, a thick column of light in which flecks of dust floated, streamed through the kitchen window. My mom sat hunched over the kitchen table engrossed in what looked to me like a pile of wastepaper. Without looking up, she sipped a glass of milk with one hand, while with the other she slowly turned the pages of something printed on long, thin, unattached sheets of paper.

"What's that?" I asked, kicking off my shoes and piling my school books on the table.

She didn't answer. In fact, she hadn't even heard me.

"What'cha reading?" I repeated.

She lifted her eyes, glanced briefly at me, and then lowered them again, returning to the heap of paper before her. Her lips moved and she mumbled something over and over again as she scanned each page. It sounded like a chant or a prayer. For several minutes I watched, perplexed and amazed. Something had come over my mother and I was dying to find out what it was. She looked peaceful and calm and almost young again. Finally, she raised her eyes above the pages and gazed out the window as if to memorize something.

"Betsy!" she exclaimed in surprise when she noticed me. "When did *you* get home?"

"I've been sitting here for a good ten minutes watching you.

What are you doing? And what is that weird pile of paper you're reading?"

"Galley proofs," she said almost proudly.

"What's that?" It sounded like kitchen duty in the army.

"Mrs. Schecter—she's in my book-discussion group—says that this is the first stage in the printing of a book." She lowered her voice as if she were confiding a secret, "A book that hasn't been published yet. Mrs. Schecter's nephew works for a big New York publishing house and he smuggled the galleys out. We're taking turns reading. The book is *won*-der-ful," she said, pronouncing every syllable. "By a woman writer named Betty Friedan."

"What's it called?"

"The Feminine Mystique."

The feminine Miss Who?" I asked.

"Mys-*tique*. Oh, Betsy, it's so exciting! I've never read anything like it. It's about me. About my problem. She calls it 'the problem that has no name.' You know, that feeling I have these days of being unhappy and bored. She says a lot of women feel the way I do. It's *'Kinder, Kuche, Kirche.'*"

I recognized the sounds my mother had been mumbling to herself as she read, but not much else. "Mom," I said, "you know I don't understand Yiddish. I don't know what you're talking about."

"It isn't Yiddish, Betsy. It's German. A Nazi slogan. It means 'Children, Kitchen, and Church.' The Nazis used it to tell German women the only three things they should do with their lives—have children, keep house, and go to church. This Betty Friedan talks about how unfair that is."

"Why? There are lots of women who are happy being housewives and mothers," I said, thinking, as I said it, how I wished my mother were one of them.

"That's true," my mother answered with excitement, "but don't you see? Now that I've read this book, I realize that it doesn't have to be the same way for everyone."

I was trying hard to see, but I still didn't know what my mother was talking about. Then I thought of Janet's mother. "Janet Bloom's mother is a lawyer," I said, not knowing why I was talking about her. "She even drives a truck."

"Well," my mother said, "she must have been an exceptionally brave young woman."

"Why?"

"Because it's hard to be different now and it was even harder when we were young. When I was growing up, all my friends and I ever thought about was getting married and raising a family. If we thought about working, it was only until we met our husbands. You were never supposed to think seriously about yourself or about working. It was only a means to an end. That was the way my mother had lived and it was the way we were taught all women should live. When I met daddy and he asked me to marry him, I felt like I had made it. Daddy's work went well, and then we had you, and then Jeannie, and it seemed as if I had everything anyone could expect out of life."

"So, what happened to change all that?" I asked, feeling angry and hurt.

"Nothing much. Only that you and Jeannie are older now and don't need me the way you used to. Daddy has his work. All I have is you. Now that you and Jeannie are more or less on your own, I have all this time and nothing to do. I have to find something new for myself. Until this book, until today, I've felt guilty for feeling the way I do and frightened about trying anything new."

"I guess I haven't encouraged you much," I said, feeling my own guilt. "I'm sorry."

"It isn't your fault," she said, reaching across the table with both hands and drawing me toward her. "It's nobody's fault. It's just the way things have been. I'm not a very courageous woman and I know I haven't been the best example to you. But somehow, despite my influence, you're already a brave young woman."

"Oh, no, mom, you said that once before to me, but you're

wrong. I'm not brave. I'm scared to do *everything*. Bernie says it's because I think too much."

"Bernie's smart," my mother interrupted.

"And brave," I added. "I'm too scared to do anything on my own. If I didn't have Bernie along with me to give me courage, I'd never do anything. I'm a real northern fried chicken."

"A what?"

"A northern fried chicken. Bernie called me that once when she was angry and then she tried to take it back, but she was right. I'm chicken about everything. Talking to boys, speaking in public, signing up for things . . ."

"I still say you're brave," my mother insisted.

"That's because you don't see me in action. My body trembles, my knees knock, I sweat. . . ."

"But, Betsy, having courage doesn't mean being unafraid. It means being able to overcome your fear and face things. It's easy to be brave when you aren't frightened, but it's something else when you're aware of your fear and still you push past it. That's the struggle I have all the time. I get frightened of something new and then I retreat. That's when you get impatient with me."

"Maybe I get impatient with you because we're so much alike."

"Maybe so. But still I watch you and you're different. You get frightened, but you don't back away."

"Well, I try not to," I said, thinking of the clipboard and the demonstration, "but I don't always succeed."

"I want you to succeed," my mother said firmly. She stared at me. "I want you to be happy in your life. I want you to be everything you want to be. I don't want you to be handicapped by fear. I want you to grow up to be whatever's right for you—a housewife, a mother, a teacher, even a stockbroker. I don't want you to wake up one day at my age, stuck."

"You're not stuck, mom," I said, almost pleading. The word sounded so short and final.

"Yes, I am."

"Then I want you to get unstuck," I said quietly.

"Thanks." My mother smiled at me. "You help me and I'll help you. We both have to be brave and dare to go farther."

"Yes," I said, catching some of her fire, "we do."

"Egg roll or wonton?" Bernie asked. Her eyes peered mysteriously over the top of the tall red menu.

"Egg roll," I answered, salivating.

It was Saturday evening and Bernie and I were having Chinese night on the town. Chinese food in a Chinese restaurant off Thayer Street and then the latest Frank Sinatra movie, *The Manchurian Candidate*, about a Chinese plot to overthrow the U.S. government.

"Fried rice?"

"Yup."

"Then what?" she asked.

"Chicken chow mein's fine with me."

"But I know what's even better," Bernie said with a gleam in her eye. She motioned to the waiter. "We'll have one order of egg rolls, one fried rice, and an order of shrimp in lobster sauce to share."

"Bernie!" I protested.

"And bring us chopsticks and extra noodles."

The waiter nodded and called to a woman at the cash register, who answered something back in Chinese.

"Bernie, why'd you do that? I didn't mind eating chow mein. I *like* it."

"Look, what my parents don't know won't hurt me. The only time I get to eat nonkosher stuff is with you. And anyway, I've had it. I'm sick of them. I'm sick of doing everything their way."

"What's the matter?" I asked.

Bernie was silent as the waiter returned. He shoved a small vase of plastic flowers to one side, poured us some tea, and set down a tin serving dish of egg rolls.

I reached for the hot mustard and put a few tiny drops of it on my plate while Bernie emptied about a third of a cup of duck sauce onto hers.

"Well, are you gonna tell me about it or not?" I asked, biting into my egg roll and letting the juicy, oily taste ooze slowly across my tongue.

Bernie shrugged. Her eyes filled with tears and she became engrossed in dissecting the insides of her egg roll. "It's Joan," she said, after a while. "She's spending the weekend at home instead of in the dorm and she's got this new boyfriend from Brown who came last night for sabbath dinner." Bernie picked up the remaining piece of egg roll and jammed it whole into her mouth.

"Well?" I asked. "What's he like?"

"Well," she said in a high, phony accent, "he's *ev-er-y*-thing. Good-looking, Jewish, and premed. I could tell—my parents were already planning Joan's wedding."

"So?"

"So, last night, after he left, they came trooping into my room for A Discussion. Joan, too. The three of them."

"All three of them? How'd they find a place to sit in all that mess?"

Bernie frowned at me. "It isn't funny. They're really angry with—"

The waiter appeared and Bernie lowered her voice. He set some rice and a large tureen down in the center of the table. Bernie lifted the top off and inhaled the steamy aroma. I took a large spoon and started dividing and serving the shrimp in lobster sauce.

"They're really angry with me," she continued when the waiter had gone. "They want me to get serious."

There was that word again—the one Bernie had used about Janet. I still didn't know what it meant. "What does 'get serious' mean?"

"It means a lot of things. For one thing, it means be more like Joan, be more of 'a lady.' "

"But you're already 'a lady,' " I said, admiring her. She was wearing a new pink and white pinstripe shirtwaist dress with a gold circle pin carefully placed on the side of her blouse that indicated she was "available." She looked starchy and pretty and grown up.

"*You* think I'm a lady, but they don't. They think only Joan's a lady and they want me to be just like her: keep my room clean, stay out of trouble, study all the time. They're afraid. Afraid that next year when I apply, I won't get into Pembroke. And I guess what they're really afraid of is that I won't meet a respectable Jewish boy like Joan's twerp from Brown."

Bernie lifted a fat pink shrimp on her chopsticks and stuffed it angrily into her mouth. "Joan is happy doing exactly what my parents want her to do. She watches out for what other people think and never does anything out of the ordinary. But I just can't be that way."

"Is that what your parents want? Is that what they say to you?"

"Not in those exact words, but in a sort of a code. It's *all* code, that be-serious bit and the be-a-lady bit, and, of course, their all-time favorite, 'be nice.' It all means the same thing, though: Do what you're told and don't make waves and you'll be happy and make us happy and end up exactly like us. Only I'm not sure yet that that's how I want to end up. All I know is I'm *sick* of being the black sheep and the odd one out in my family."

Bernie's eyes clouded over and she reached for the serving spoon and started spooning up and gulping down all the lobster sauce that remained in the tureen. When she had lapped up the very last of the sauce, she asked, "Have you had enough?"

"Nice of you to think of me," I said.

Bernie's eyes cleared and she noticed the empty tureen. It looked like it had been licked clean by a voracious dog. "Sorry," she said with embarrassment. "I got carried away." She jumped up suddenly from the table. "Be right back. I'm going to the ladies' room."

In a second she had gone and left me to chase the last shrimp around my plate and call for a check. The waiter cleared the table and brought the bill and two fortune cookies. I poured some tea and waited for Bernie to emerge from the bathroom.

Four or five minutes went by, and finally she appeared with freshly teased hair and a competely new makeup job. It was obvious that she'd been crying and that she was trying to hide it.

"Are you okay?" I asked.

Bernie merely nodded.

"Well then," I said, trying to cheer her up, "what are you trying to do? Show me up?" I glanced down at the stretched-out blue pullover and the plain gray skirt I was wearing. "You'll be the best-looking female in the movie house. Maybe they'll turn up the lights so that everyone can see you."

"Maybe . . ." Bernie said. She looked strange. She had a distant look in her eyes. "Come on," she said, "let's get out of here. Let's go."

"Okay." I reached for the check. "Give me a dollar fifty and we're even." Bernie handed me some money and we got up to leave.

Outside, she started up the motor of her parents' car and pulled silently out of the parking spot.

"The movie's supposed to be scary. Do you think I'll end up watching it through my fingers?" I asked.

Bernie didn't answer. It was almost as if she hadn't heard me.

"Bernie?"

"What?"

"Hey, Bernie," I said, "are you sure you're okay? You just missed the right turn for downtown."

Again Bernie didn't answer. She just kept driving straight down Thayer Street. Without blinking. It was as if she were in some kind of a trance.

"Where do you think you're going, Bernie?" I asked with concern. We were stopped at a red light at the corner of the Brown University campus.

Bernie turned slowly toward me and opened her mouth to say something. Her eyes didn't focus. She seemed to be looking through me. "Bernie?" I pleaded. "Are you all right?" I felt frightened. The horn on the car behind us belched out a warning blast. The light had turned green and Bernie hadn't budged. "Do you want me to drive?"

"No," Bernie said vaguely. "We're going to have some fun tonight." She started the car up again and we crept slowly down Thayer Street, inching along the edge of the Brown campus in the big black Buick like a huge, prowling animal.

Along the curb, some Brown boys were sitting drinking their Saturday-night cans of beer. They hooted at us as we passed. Bernie pushed a button on the dashboard and the front windows rolled open automatically.

"Bernie! What are you doing?" I yelled.

I startled her. She jumped and appeared to come out of her trance. "We're going to have an adventure," she said. "As long as they don't think I'm serious or a lady, I might as well enjoy myself."

"But, Bernie," I protested.

She ignored me, turning down the back of the Brown campus and crawling even more slowly along. The speedometer vibrated back and forth somewhere between four and five miles per hour. The dark street came alive with boys. From every niche and nook, boys, like insects, emerged and swarmed toward us. Each cluster of boys was drunker and crazier than the last. They wove in and out of the street in small circles, clutching their beer cans and each other, rocking back

70

and forth on their heels. It seemed inevitable that we would hit one of them, but Bernie deftly steered and swerved the car out of their way.

I flattened myself against the back of my seat, legs and arms extended to absorb the impact of a sudden crash. "Bernie, *please,* " I begged, but Bernie only laughed a strange laugh as she maneuvered ever more slowly through the crowds.

"Townies!" someone yelled, and there was a great deal of hooting and hollering. A tall redheaded boy with a matching face grabbed on to the front of the car and peered through the window at me, calling out to his friends, "Look what's here!"

I reached for the lock buttons, pushed them down, and raised the window. But it was hopeless. Bernie, with her master control panel, rolled the window down again. There were boys everywhere. About five of them piled onto the hood. Bernie jammed on her brakes and we lurched to a stop. For the moment, even she looked frightened. She pushed the panel again and the windows closed, nearly slicing the arm off a brute of a boy who grinned stupidly at me through the window. We were completely surrounded. Like animals in a cage at the zoo.

"Oh, Bernie!" It was all I could say. I was shaking and terrified. Bernie had switched off the motor, but even so, the car was jolting up and down under the weight of the boys. Someone was sitting on the roof; his brown loafers knocked against the windshield.

"What should we do?" Bernie asked quietly. She seemed to be back to herself.

"Do! Are you *asking me?*" I was outraged. Outside, boys were slapping and gesturing at the windows, trying to get us to open them. "I thought you wanted an adventure!"

"I do," Bernie said, with determination. "But this is too much." She looked almost as frightened as I was.

I sat stiffly in my seat in the center of the car away from the window, keeping my eyes directed at the carpet in front of me. "There's nothing to do except sit here and hope they go away. Just don't encourage any of them by looking their way." From the corner of my eye, I watched Bernie lower her eyes and stare at the floor.

We sat for what seemed like forever, not moving a muscle, occasionally shifting our eyes from side to side, taking note first of each other and then of the chaos outside. After a long while, the noise and the bouncing subsided.

"Should I start the car up?" Bernie asked me under her breath.

"Okay," I hissed, and dared to raise my head. Most of the boys had cleared away and only a handful were left near the car. Some of them actually seemed sober and appeared to be merely curious as to what we were doing stopped in the middle of the street. A good-looking boy in a gray jacket rapped on Bernie's window and Bernie lowered the glass about an inch to hear what he was saying.

"Can I help you?" he asked, in perfect, unslurred speech.

"No, thanks, it's okay now," Bernie said, and smiled at him.

"I don't suppose you'd be interested in a drink or a cup of coffee? My dorm has open house tonight."

Bernie glanced nervously at me. Then she turned toward the boy. "Sure, why not?"

"Bernie!" I gasped.

"I can't help it," she whispered apologetically. "You take the car. I'll find a way to get home myself."

"But *why*, Bernie? *Why?*"

"I don't know. I don't know," she repeated. "I can't help it." She looked as if she were about to cry, as if she were drowning.

"I'll go with you," I offered.

"No, I have to do this myself. Alone." She unlocked the door, lifted the handle, and got out of the car. A loud whoop went up from the remaining boys. The boy in the jacket smiled strangely and hung his arm around Bernie as if she belonged to him.

I slid quickly over to the driver's seat and locked the door.

"Bernie," I called, starting to cry. "What shall I tell your parents?"

Bernie leaned close to the partly open window. "Tell them . . . tell them I went to find a husband." I looked closely at her face and saw that she, too, was crying, but before I could say anything more, the boy pulled her away from the car and walked her across the street into the shadows.

Some of the other boys were starting to surround the car again, calling out to me. "Hey, townie! Want to go for a ride?"

I drew in my breath, shifted the car out of park, pressed the accelerator pedal to the floor, and took off down the street, watching the needle on the speedometer move from five to ten to twenty to thirty miles an hour. I didn't exhale until fifteen minutes later when I screeched into the driveway at Bernie's house. There was a light on in the kitchen window, but it was obvious no one was home. Except for the creaking of the trees, it was perfectly still. Itzhak's green eyes glowed from behind a trash can. I sat for a minute in the car, thinking, and then grabbed a pen and a scrap of paper from my handbag and scribbled a quick note:

Bernie and an old friend went out for coffee. She'll be back later,

Betsy

It was the best I could do. I shoved it under the back door and ran all the way home in tears.

"I wonder what they're discussing," Bernie said suspiciously.

It was one month later and we stood at the door of the Meeting Hall, waiting for Neil Segal to call the latest meeting of PROJECT to order. He and Janet Bloom were off to one side talking.

"I don't know," I answered. Bernie's tone annoyed me. Since the night of the great adventure, something had changed between us and now almost everything she said annoyed me. Maybe we could have cleared things up between us by talking about them, but whenever I asked her about the night at Brown, Bernie changed the subject. And, as usual, I was too chicken to press her about it or to tell her how angry I felt. Her parents, who were as much in the dark as I was, had nevertheless grounded Bernie for several weeks "on principle."

Bernie was a model daughter now. She had always studied, but now she studied harder. Even her room was neat; at least it seemed to be. At the end of each day, she stuffed her clothes into the closet or under the bed. She even changed Itzhak's litter box. We saw each other for shorter and shorter periods of time now. Bernie was always busy. Studying Hebrew, doing homework, cleaning up. Bernie had decided to please her parents and there was no stopping her.

"God! Am I thirsty!" Bernie said too loudly. Her elbow was

back in its favorite position, nestled deep against my small intestine, and her pupils were making wide circles around her eyes.

"What *is* it?" I asked feeling annoyed again. I turned to glare at her and saw that, out of nowhere, Kenny Klein had appeared and was standing by my side.

"Excuse me while I find the bubbler. I'm positively dying of thirst," Bernie said, with a little too much enthusiasm. Before I could stop her, she disappeared into the crowd.

I shifted my eyes away from Kenny Klein and started studying the floor and the pattern the black and white linoleum tiles made.

"She's not terribly subtle, that Bernie," I heard Kenny say.

"No, she isn't."

"It's just as well, though. I'd rather talk to you alone."

"Please?" I couldn't believe what I thought he'd said.

"I wanted to ask you if you'd like to go out next weekend. I don't know if you like basketball or not, but I have tickets for a Friars' game Saturday night and I thought that maybe you'd like to go? Afterward, we could get something to eat—you know, at Greg's or at the Tête-à-tête?"

I was speechless.

"Betsy? Of course, if you don't like basketball—"

"Basketball!" I squeaked. "Fast break, full court press, dunk!" Why was I standing there like a total idiot rattling off every basketball term I'd ever heard? I simply had to grab hold of myself. "One on one," I heard myself say.

"Right," Kenny mumbled vaguely. It was clear that he didn't know what had come over me. "Well, how about it?"

"Sure, I'd *love* to!" I wanted to hug him for making me feel so happy. "Who're they playing?" I asked, as if it mattered.

"St. John's." Kenny seemed pleased. "I'll pick you up at seven. Mayflower Avenue, right?"

"Right." How long had he known *that?* I wondered.

"Okay, see you then." People were taking their seats and Kenny hurried over to Neil and Janet and left me standing alone, like a lamp, lighting up the world around me.

"I heard it all," Bernie whispered in my ear, and squeezed me. "I *told* you he liked you."

I just nodded and let Bernie lead me, like a pull toy, to a seat.

Neil banged his hammer and the meeting began. In a half-conscious state, I watched Kenny and Neil administer the opening proceedings. The score was 65 to 62 and the Friars were taking a free throw when I heard Janet say my name. She had come to the part in the minutes of the previous meeting that included my description of the Food for Freedom day.

"You're blushing," Bernie whispered.

I didn't need her to tell me. I already knew. I could feel my forehead burning.

Janet finished her report and then said that she had an announcement to make. "Neil and I are about to make the arrangements for our annual interfaith meeting, which is scheduled for next month. We have decided to invite a Negro church group, the Paradise Baptist Church Fellowship, to attend our next meeting. . . ."

"I wish it were Charlayne Perry's group," I whispered to Bernie.

". . . What we want to discuss now is what to do. Neil had what I think is a good idea. He suggested a dance. Are there any other suggestions or is everyone in favor of Neil's suggestion for a dance?"

Janet looked out over the sea of heads, waiting for a hand to go up, but not a single one did. In fact, except for the shifting of feet, the Meeting Hall was strangely quiet.

Neil rose to his feet, hammer in hand. "Since no one has any other suggestions," he said, "I take it that everyone's in agreement that we have a dance next month with the Paradise Baptist Church Fellowship." He raised the hammer and was about to slam it down on his block of wood when someone called out from the back of the room.

Stanley Katz, the boy who Janet said had worked on the Food for Freedom day, stood up. "I'm not sure," he said slowly, "that a dance is the best idea. After all, we'll be strangers. It might be a better idea to have an opportunity to talk, to get to know one another—you know, one to one. Perhaps, instead of a dance, it would be a better idea to have some refreshments and just circulate."

"I agree," another voice called out.

But then Sally Axelrod, the girl Janet had been talking to at the last meeting, stood up. "I disagree. What's better than a dance for getting to know people? I think it's an excellent idea and we should do it."

There was a lot of mumbled sound, but no one spoke up.

"Anyone else?" Janet asked.

"Why, yes," Kenny said. He spoke, without standing, from his seat at her elbow. "I've given this some thought and I'm afraid I don't think a dance is a good idea. How about something more along the lines of a discussion of some topical issue. The problem of civil rights in the South? The recent situation with James Meredith? I think the dance idea is out of place."

"How so?" Neil asked.

"I just think that holding a dance with them isn't a good idea."

"Why not?" someone challenged from the audience. It was cookie-faced Mickey Epstein. "What's the matter with *them?*" he asked, leaning on the last word.

"Nothing," Kenny answered. "Except that—well— everyone knows that they're different from us. They'd be the first to agree."

"Yes!" someone shouted, and suddenly there was an explosion of sound as people began talking and yelling back and forth to one another.

"When you get right down to it," La Princesse said, pronouncing each word distinctly, "they're black and we're white."

"You can't argue with that!" someone else yelled.

There was a lot of laughter, but I couldn't figure out who was on whose side. I wiped some dampness from my forehead. Even though the room was cool, I had started to perspire.

Stanley Katz rose to his feet again. "Look, let's not kid ourselves. This equality business can only go so far. Kenny's right, we're just not the same."

"Bernie!" I said. "Did you *hear* what he said? And he collected food for Food for Freedom. How can that be?"

Bernie didn't answer. She sat, folded up and tiny, shoulders hunched and head fixed and lowered, looking neither right nor left.

"It seems to me," Carol Schwartz said, "that the issue is no longer whether or not we should have a dance, it's the bigotry here in this room."

"That's right," some voices yelled. Up front, Janet and Neil nodded in agreement.

"It's not bigotry," Sybil Kaye called out breathlessly. "I don't have to dance with them just to prove that we're equal. I can talk with them. I think we should have a discussion instead."

A lot of people murmured and some shouted their agreement.

"Bernie!" I said. "What's going on here? Has everyone gone crazy?"

Bernie seemed to shrink even farther away from me into her chair.

"Bernie? What's happening? Stanley Katz, Sybil Kaye, Penny Prince, even Kenny Klein! Carol Schwartz is right. They *are* a bunch of bigots. Bernie!" I shouted angrily when she still didn't answer. "Where *are* you?"

"Shhhhhhhhh," she said. " You always get so excited. Calm down." And suddenly, although I was perspiring, my body trembled with cold.

"I think Carol and some of the rest of you are overstating the case when you call this discussion 'bigotry,' " Kenny said calmly. "You're right, though, the issue isn't a dance, it's what a dance means. It's what Penny Prince said: We're different—they're black and we're white. Equality's fine, but just think about it. What would your parents say if you came home next month and told them that you'd just danced with a Negro?"

There was something about the way he said the words "a Negro" that got to me. Something about the way he sat there in his neat clothes with his neat features pronouncing those words in such an even, distanced way that both sickened and infuriated me. I thought of Charlayne and felt embarrassed. It was as if she were watching and listening to all of this.

"And how would *you* feel," Kenny continued, "if you'd just danced with a Negro?"

There they were again, those words. They made me feel hot and agitated and nervous. Like a pot about to boil over. "I'd feel fine!" I yelled, leaping to my feet. "Who do you think you are, talking like that? What is this 'us' and 'them' business? I thought we were all the same." My body twitched with excitement. I sat back down in my chair. I couldn't believe that I'd jumped up and spoken out like that. I didn't know what had come over me. And the strangest thing of all was that instead of feeling frightened or embarrassed, I felt energized. As if there were a kind of fire burning inside me, one that gave me strength.

Kenny stared at me. He was startled. "You're overly excited, Betsy. You've misunderstood me. All I meant was something simple. Look, you all know how I feel about them. They should be allowed to vote, they should be allowed to ride buses with us, they should be allowed to eat in restaurants with us. But, Betsy," he said, lowering his voice to a near whisper, "would you want to go out with one of them?"

I looked straight at Kenny, sitting there in his pressed chinos with the perfect crease down the middle and his perfectly clean green crew-neck sweater and his perfect face, and I felt disgusted. I jumped to my feet to answer him, but suddenly I felt an arm trying to pull me down. "Don't," Bernie said. She was pleading. I looked down at her, huddled in her chair, wanting to keep me quiet, trying to keep me down when there I was, so angry and outraged that I had finally lost all my fear. I felt betrayed. I wrenched myself free of Bernie and stood up straight.

"I'm asking you, Betsy. Would you go out with one of them?" Kenny repeated.

"Sooner than I'd go out with you," I hissed, and then burst into tears.

There was a great hush across the room as everyone stopped talking and arguing and sat waiting to see what would happen next. I felt naked and terribly alone. Kenny's face had turned pale and he looked away from me.

"You're all hypocrites!" I shouted. "I can't believe this. I just can't believe this. I thought this kind of thing only happened in the South. How stupid I've been! I thought minorities supported other minorities. What about Food for Freedom? I thought Jews were always there for those who are oppressed. Have you forgotten who you are? People used to say things like that about us. That we were different. One minute it was that; and the next, they were sending us off to concentration camps to die. Look," I said. I ran to the back of the room where Mr. Trachtenberg, the janitor, was standing. I tugged at his sleeve. "Show them your arm. Show them the number on your arm. Remind them. They seem to have forgotten." Mr. Trachtenberg was very shy, but nevertheless he cooperated. He walked slowly to the front of the room and rolled up his sleeve until the ugly ink-gray tattoo of his concentration-camp number was visible.

"She's right!" someone shouted.

The room grew completely still. I could hear people breathing.

"What's going on here?" I yelled. "I don't understand how any of you can be unsympathetic to a Negro or a Catholic or to anyone else who is in a minority." I was crying loudly now, deep heaves of pain. I felt so many things. Bewilderment, disappointment, anger, hurt, and, curiously enough, release.

Neil banged his hammer and I looked up and saw that he and Janet were standing.

"Look, maybe we should wrap this up now. Take a vote," Neil called out.

There was a lot of murmuring in response.

"Shall we do a voice vote?" Janet asked.

"Yes," several people called out.

"Okay," Neil said, standing. "All those in favor of holding a dance with the Paradise Baptist Church Fellowship, say 'aye.' "

"Aye!" I yelled at the top of my lungs, and my voice combined with many others. I looked over at Bernie. She had neither voted nor moved.

"All those opposed, say 'nay,' " Neil said.

"Nay," the clear majority rang out.

Again Bernie just sat there.

"The nays have it," Neil said. "There will be no dance with the members of the Paradise Baptist Church."

There was a lot of angry muttering and a small amount of applause.

"I move that we postpone our annual interfaith meeting until such time as we find an appropriate entertainment with which the majority of the membership concurs. Does anyone second my motion?" Neil asked. He sounded tired.

"Seconded," someone called out.

Suddenly everyone was talking at once to one another, trying to make sense out of what had happened. Bernie and I just looked at each other. It was as if I were seeing her for the very first time. I thought about what I'd done. Part of me felt like I'd made a fool of myself, but another part felt strong and sure of herself in a way it had never felt before.

"Bernie," I cried, *"why did you try to stop me?* Was it what I was saying or the way I said it?"

"Some of both," Bernie answered quietly.

"Why didn't you vote?" I asked.

Bernie merely shrugged.

I looked at her sitting there, small and scared in her too-fancy clothes, and I felt furious.

"Then you're the biggest hypocrite of all!" I said. "You who always told me to stop being scared. I finally do and you try to keep me from speaking out! I looked up to you, Bernie. I looked up to you! I thought you were brave!" I was crying again, but outrage quickly drove the tears away.

"And the Food for Freedom thing! Now I *know* why you

don't like Janet Bloom and why you were so suspicious of Charlayne Perry. It isn't the great Betsy Andbernie friendship, it's bigotry! You're just like Kenny Klein and Stanley Katz and some of the others. Everything is one big social event until it gets too close for comfort. Food for Freedom! You just go along for the ride—dress right and maybe you'll meet someone, and then as soon as you do, you disappear. Well, you can have your Barf Manley and you can get someone else to accompany you on your night escapades to Brown. I've had enough. No more Betsy Andbernie. From now on, it's me, Betsy Bergman. By herself!"

Thick teardrops rolled slowly down Bernie's face, leaving gray pathmarks from her mascara. "Please," she breathed, "no more!"

"Yes," I said, unable to stop myself. "No more."

Neil banged his hammer again and everyone quieted down while Janet spoke. "The demonstration in favor of the housing project is next month at two o'clock at the Roger Williams Monument on Prospect Terrace. A number of you have signed up for it already, but if there are any others who wish to do so, the list will be up here and you can add your name."

Neil made a motion to adjourn the meeting and Kenny seconded it. With a lot of scraping, everyone pushed their chairs back and got up to talk, stretch, and get some refreshments.

I stood up and looked at Bernie. She sat still in her seat, staring intently at me, looking as if she wanted very badly to say something. I opened my mouth to speak to her, but nothing came out. There was nothing more to say. Someone tapped me on the shoulder.

"You were fantastic," Sally Axelrod said.

"You were," Mickey Epstein added.

"Yes," someone I didn't know said.

"Thanks." I pushed past them. I didn't want to be complimented—and besides, something was propelling me up, out of my seat, away from Bernie and forward to the front of the room. I tried to think what it was, but my mind was a blank. All I could see in the blankness was the inexplicable image of my mother's face watching me. The strange force pushed me past groups of people, many of whom paused in their conversation to stare at me. It didn't let me stop until I had reached the table where Kenny, Neil, and Janet stood talking to one another.

"I want to sign the list," I said as soon as I got there. The words seemed to fall out as if they were too heavy to stay inside. I looked up and found myself gazing directly into Kenny Klein's face.

"Here it is," he said, handing me Janet's clipboard in an awkward sort of way.

I took it from him, lowered my eyes, and leaned over to sign my name. My palm was sweating and my fingers trembled as I tried to maneuver the pen and avoid his glance.

"I guess we'd better forget about that game," I heard him say. But by the sound of his voice, it was hard to tell whether he was asking me or telling me.

"Guess so," I said, still not looking up. I was all mixed up. A minute ago I'd been flying because at long last Kenny Klein had asked me out. Now, in an instant, everything had changed. I wished I could turn back the clock to when everything had seemed so simple. Was this what growing up was about? If so, it was awfully hard. I felt Kenny move away from me and I dared to raise my eyes. Janet smiled at me.

"I'm glad you decided to go."

"Me, too," I said. Inside, my mother's face broke into a smile.

"It was awful today. I wish it had never happened. But you were wonderful—what you said, the way you—"

"No, I wasn't," I interrupted, not knowing what I was about to say. "I'm all emotion, no facts. Either I'm frightened or I'm angry. I wanted to say all kinds of things—about the slaves, about the Civil War, about history—but I don't know facts. I just exploded, that's all. I didn't think first and then speak. I felt first and then. . . ."

"You're like my mom," Janet smiled.

"I am?"

"She's got a terrible temper." Janet winced a little. "That's why she decided to become a lawyer. Now the big word in her life is 'rational.' She's always trying to be 'rational.' "

"Your mother is wonderful."

"I know," Janet said, but then she frowned. "She wants me to follow in her footsteps and become a lawyer."

"Are you going to?"

"Not if I can help it. Her footsteps are too big. They make me feel sometimes as if I don't know who I am." Janet pulled a small piece of paper from her clipboard and handed it to me. It was the poem she had written. "Look at this."

"I confess. I've already read that," I said with embarrassment.

"Oh." Her voice was shy. "Then you know how I feel. . . . Do you want to go together to the demonstration?"

"Sure," I answered.

"My mom's going, too. We'll pick you up."

"Great," I said. "Maybe—"

"Betsy?" a familiar voice interrupted.

Bernie stood awkwardly to one side. Her eyes were red. Janet excused herself and moved discreetly away.

"What is it?" I asked suspiciously. She looked as if she wanted to apologize or make up or something.

"Nothing," Bernie said shyly. "I just wondered what happened with Kenny. You *are* going to go out with him, aren't you? I mean, you didn't really mean what you said to him, did you?"

I couldn't believe my ears. This was positively the last straw. "Of all the things to say!" I exploded. "Of all the things to ask about! Is that the only thing that interests you? How is it possible that we've been friends, let alone best friends?"

Bernie didn't move, but her whole body seemed to shrink from me. "I was just trying to—to—to get you to—speak to—"

"Friendship circle!" Neil called out, banging on a glass. Friendship circle, I thought. The whole thing was absurd.

"I'm getting out of here," I yelled to Bernie. "I don't belong and I don't *want* to belong."

I ran out of the Meeting Hall into the cloakroom and collapsed against a coatrack. I felt exhausted with all the emotion of the last few hours. I sat down on the floor and took some deep breaths and tried to pull myself together. Walk, I thought. Walk home and walk this whole business off. I stood up, grabbed my coat, and headed into the lobby toward the front door.

The door to the Meeting Hall was open and through it I could see everyone standing, arms braided in a circle. They were singing.

> We shall overcome
> We shall overcome
> We shall overcome
> Some day.
> Oh, deep in my heart
> I do believe
> We shall overcome
> Some day.
>
> We'll walk hand in hand
> We'll walk hand in hand
> We'll walk hand in hand
> One day.
> Oh, deep in my heart
> I do believe
> We'll walk hand in hand
> One day.©

Hypocrites, I thought. Hypocrites! I leaned against the heavy wooden doors and pushed my way out.

12

Three weeks later, on a Saturday afternoon, Janet and Frieda picked me up to drive me to the demonstration.

"Tell her," Janet's mother said as I climbed into the back seat and slammed the door.

Mrs. Bloom switched off the motor.

"Tell her what?" I asked, uncomfortably.

Janet was wearing an old loden coat. She fiddled with the buttons and wouldn't look at me. "The organizers of the demonstration tried to get a permit but it didn't come through. The word is there may be trouble."

"What kind of trouble?" I asked.

"A counterdemonstration. We're not sure," Frieda said. "But the demonstration is now against the law, and if you participate in it, you'll be *breaking* the law."

"Civil disobedience," I said, suddenly comprehending the meaning of that term.

"Exactly," Frieda said. "It's up to you."

She and Janet sat still, awaiting my answer. I could feel their eyes on me as I tried to figure out what to do.

Civil disobedience, I thought, that was something they practiced down south, not up north. What had happened to Charlayne's friends couldn't possibly happen here. But then, I wasn't at all sure. Who were the counterdemonstrators? Did they wear white sheets like the Ku Klux Klan? I was surely getting carried away. There was nothing to be afraid of, here in the North, I thought, but even as I reassured myself, the northern fried chicken in me rose up and started fluttering its wings. I was scared. Really scared. I wanted to turn to Bernie and ask her what to do. But there was no Bernie anymore. There hadn't been for weeks. It was up to me. I was on my own. I had to make a decision by myself. And I knew what I had to do.

"Okay," I said finally, exhaling and blowing out some of my tension. "I'm chicken but I'll go."

"Great!" Janet and Frieda shouted in one breath. Janet's mother gunned the motor and we were off.

"What's this demonstration about, anyway?" I felt embarrassed by my ignorance. Why was I always so big on feelings and so short on facts?

Janet's mother's smile reassured me. It was as if we were old friends. "Do you know about the bill President Kennedy signed into law saying that all housing built with federal funds must be integrated?"

"A little," I lied, thinking I really had to start reading the newspaper.

"Well, the Lincoln Hill Housing Project is being built with federal funds and the people who live in the neighborhood are frightened. They've gotten together and formed an organization called the Lincoln Hill Improvement Society. They say they want to improve the neighborhood, but what they really want is to keep Negroes out and to stop the project from being built."

"But that's horrible!" I said.

"Horrible," Janet's mother said, "but inevitable. Most people are frightened of differences."

"That's the problem with some of the people down south," Janet said.

"Along with some of the people up north," I said, thinking of the PROJECT meeting.

"And the problem with people in the past," Janet's motner added, signaling a left turn. "When *I* was a kid, Catholics were afraid of Jews, and Jews were afraid of Catholics."

"You're kidding! I really don't know very much about the world."

"You'll learn," Janet's mother laughed. She pulled into a spot on Prospect Street and switched off the motor. "Well, here we are," she announced. In a second she was out of the car and walking up Cushing Street on the way to Congdon, with Janet and me following close behind. Just ahead of us was Prospect Terrace.

On normal days it's an empty, peaceful spot; a few people read papers on the benches, someone admires the view, a young mother wheels a carriage. But today things were different. Though it was only ten minutes to two, already there were close to a hundred people crowded into the tiny park.

I wondered why the organizers of the demonstration had picked this small, out-of-the-way spot. The terrace sits high on a hill overlooking the city. From it you can stand looking out across downtown Providence and the world beyond it like the ruler of a kingdom. The snow-white dome of the state capitol gleams against the blue sky and the city looks both miniature and infinite at the same time. On the edge of the terrace, watching over the city like a kind and concerned father, is a huge statue of Roger Williams, who came to Rhode Island seeking religious freedom. Maybe the organizers of the demonstration thought everyone should be reminded that Rhode Island originated as a place of refuge and freedom. Maybe that was it. I wasn't sure.

People were moving in a slow, thick circle around the park. There was an eerie stillness; so many bodies, so little noise. The sound of feet scuffing against pavement, an occasional cough, a few murmurs; other than that, there was no sound.

For a few minutes Janet, Frieda, and I stood on the periphery of the crowd and watched. An old Negro man with skin like dried leaves carried a hand-lettered piece of cardboard that read, "We Can't Wait. Freedom Now." A young girl with thick blond braids waved a sign at the end of a long wooden stick that said, "Good Christians Come in Every Color. Equal Housing for All." Across the way, a Negro boy about my age held a wide band of paper in two hands that read, "Freedom in the South *AND* Freedom in the North." In the distance I recognized Mickey Epstein walking with a boy I'd never seen before. He was carrying a homemade sign in the shape and design of an equality button, a white equal sign painted on a black disk.

Janet's mother glanced quickly at us and we stepped toward the demonstration. In a second, the crowd silently opened, like a huge embrace, and took us in. We shuffled along, inching forward, unable, because of lack of space, to take anything but the tiniest of steps. All at once I felt part of a wonderful machine, its axles, gears, and pistons all working together to push it steadily forward. An early-spring breeze blew across my face and took the chill out of the air and I felt warm and enclosed as I circled slowly around the terrace, in and out of the shadow of Roger Williams.

Ahead of me someone began humming the melody to "We Shall Overcome," and soon all of us joined in. The singing was rich with the sound of voices of all kinds mixed together. I sang out softly at first and then louder and louder, "We are not afra-ay-aid. We are not afra-ay-aid. We are not afraid today-ay-ay-ay. Oh-woe deep in my heart, I do believe, we shall overcome some day."

Janet held my left hand and someone reached out on my right side and clasped my right hand.

"Betsy," a voice drawled. "Janet."

"Charlayne!" I breathed. I turned to embrace her and was suddenly sandwiched between Janet and Charlayne in a giant, dancing, three-way hug that threatened to hold up the demonstration. We pulled apart and Charlayne tugged a hello at Janet's mother's coat sleeve and fell in with us.

"What do you think?" she asked.

"It's great!" I said.

"Yup. It's a good one," Charlayne answered in that soft, slow way of hers. "Look over there." She pointed to a young woman who was standing on the sidelines with a stenographer's pad in her hand, interviewing one of the demonstrators and taking notes. On the lapel of her trench coat she wore a badge that said PRESS.

"Is this gonna be in the papers?" I asked.

"Looks that way," Charlayne said. She seemed pleased.

Suddenly I felt self-conscious. I followed straighter and more carefully behind the people in front of me. But as the march circled for perhaps the twentieth time away from the back of the terrace and toward the street, I saw that in fact we *were* being watched.

A small group of people had gathered on the sidewalk that edged the terrace. I couldn't make out yet just what they were doing, but I noticed that as the column of demonstrators passed by, it seemed to arch away from the crowd almost the way an animal does when it senses danger.

Up ahead, people had stopped singing and as we drew closer I heard a confused mixture of sounds from the group on the sidewalk. At first I couldn't make out their words, but then suddenly it was no longer necessary to rely on my ears. Bobbing in the breeze over the heads of the street crowd was the first of several signs. "Niggers Go Home," it said. All the muscles in my body tightened and next to me I felt Charlayne and Janet stiffen. The bones in Janet's mother's face became more pronounced as she took notice of the sign. "Keep Our Schools and Neighborhoods Clean and White," another sign said. Underneath it, a large woman stood carrying a small smiling child. In its tiny hands it held a sign with the words "Keep Them Out" printed on it.

As we drew closer to the crowd, I was able to make sense out of the jumble of angry sounds. Most of the people were chanting "Stay home. Stay home. Stay home" at the demonstrators. But a few were yelling at specific people as they passed. "Stick with your own kind," one of them yelled at a Negro man a few feet in front of me. "Stay where you belong."

Closer and closer we came to the group of people on the sidewalk. In the street behind it, more and more cars were pulling up and discharging passengers, all of whom joined the crowd, until it bulged and swelled, spilling out onto the street. I was frightened and I gripped Janet's and Charlayne's hands tightly as we passed by. Out of the crowd, the woman with the baby stepped forward and pointed directly at me and Janet. "Look!" she yelled. "Look at the nigger lovers. Look at the little lily-white nigger lovers!"

My whole body began to shake with rage. Every curse word I'd ever known jumped to my lips and it was all I could do to force them back in again. "Shut up!" I screamed. "You—you—you're poison—that's what you are! Poison! And you're poisoning your baby. You ought to be—"

"Take it easy," Janet whispered to me, grabbing me by the waist and pulling me toward her.

"Just keep marching," Charlayne said tightly under her breath. She grabbed my hand. "They're baiting you. They *want* you to get angry and do something."

Janet's mother nodded to me; and Janet and Charlayne, arms around my waist, carried me forcibly forward until we had left the angry crowd a distance behind us.

Charlayne started singing:

> Oh, freedom, Oh, freedom
> Oh, freedom over me, over me
> And before I'll be a slave,
> I'll be buried in my grave
> And go home to my Lord
> And be free.
> No more segregation
> No more segregation
> No more segregation over me, over me
> And before I'll be a slave,
> I'll be buried in my grave
> And go home to my Lord
> And be free. . . .

Janet and her mother and everyone else joined in, but I couldn't get myself to sing. It was clear to me that Charlayne was singing away her anger, but I knew that tactic wouldn't work for me. I looked back over my shoulder at the crowd. They were shouting at the marchers behind us. With each shout they seemed to get more and more excited and more and more confident. They occupied all of the sidewalk, some of the street, and now they were creeping onto the terrace itself.

Off in the distance I heard the long, wounded scream of a siren approaching.

"The police," Janet murmured. All around me, heads turned in the direction of the siren. The scream grew louder and louder until it overwhelmed the singing and the shouting.

A minute or two later, four squad cars and a police van screeched to a stop in the street, scattering some of the people who were standing nearby. The noise of the siren abruptly stopped and the silence that enveloped us was intense and uncomfortable. I looked at Janet, her mother, and Charlayne, and they looked nervously back at me. "What's going to happen?" I whispered, wanting them to reassure me.

Frieda just shook her head ever so slightly from side to side. "I don't know," she said quietly.

The police poured out of their cars and dispersed themselves among us, carrying their nightsticks horizontally in front of them between two fists. The late afternoon sun sent beams of light glancing off the metal of the guns riding on their hips.

Several police assembled side by side, nightsticks raised in a chest-high chain, and formed a wedge in front of the street crowd. "Okay, folks, get back! Get back now!" they shouted, coaxing and pushing the counterdemonstrators off the sidewalk, out of the traffic, and finally back onto the pavement on the opposite side of the street.

"Get lost," a man shouted, but everyone else cooperated. When they had all been successfully pushed across the street, the police stood, backs to the crowd, in an uncrossable wall, facing us. The crowd, behind it, resumed its shouting.

"Stay home. Stay home. Stay home," they chanted.

We continued to circle slowly and uneasily around the terrace. I couldn't stop thinking, What's going to happen next? What's going to happen? No one sang. No one breathed. The remaining police stood close by, watching us, nightsticks in their hands, waiting, it seemed, for some kind of instructions.

"Attention, attention," a voice called out. It crackled like cellophane through a bullhorn.

"Here it comes," Janet whispered to her mother.

"What?" I asked, scared.

Janet nodded in the direction of a police officer who was standing on one of the park benches.

"You are in violation," he said. "I repeat—you are in violation."

I stopped moving to listen. We all did.

"This is an unlawful assembly. You have no permit. You are ordered to cease this gathering and to disperse. I repeat—this is an unlawful assembly. You must leave—you must disperse from this area."

"Yeah, go home," they shouted from across the street, cheering. "Go home where you belong."

"You have five minutes to clear this area," the voice ordered. "Anyone unwilling to cooperate will be arrested."

For a moment there was silence. I didn't dare to move. In the distance I heard the crazy singing of the starlings as they began their evening visit to the roofs and ledges of the office buildings downtown.

"It's not fair," I hissed under my breath. "What about them? How come they have the right to demonstrate and we don't?"

"You have no permit," the officer repeated as if in answer. "You have five minutes to clear this area."

From the other side of the terrace, someone started singing and clapping in rhythm. Soon Janet, Charlayne, Frieda, and everyone else joined in.

> We shall not, we shall not be moved.
> We shall not, we shall not be moved.
> Just like a tree that's planted by the water
> We shall not be moved.

At first I didn't know the words; but as they were sung over and over, I quickly caught on. I sang out. It was like throwing a dare at the police, daring them to make us leave.

I was scared but at the same time exhilarated. Kind of the way I used to feel when I was a kid and stuck my tongue out at a bully to yell, "Sticks and stones may break my bones, but words will never harm me," and then waited to see if the bully would beat me up or shrug and go away.

"Three minutes," the officer repeated through the bullhorn. "You have three minutes to clear this area."

I just kept singing and clapping along with everyone else, faster and faster until my palms began to ache and my voice felt as if it would give out.

I looked up at the sky. The setting sun, like a deflating balloon, hung suspended over the city at eye level. The police squinted past it, carefully watching us; and then, like soldiers in a perfectly straight line, took three steps toward us.

"Two minutes."

My heart was pounding. I stopped singing and noticed that the song had grown thinner. Around me, everyone was shifting about and mumbling. A few people, and then more and more, were breaking from our group, scattering and hurrying into the street, away from the demonstration. I looked back and forth from Janet to her mother to Charlayne. They, too, had stopped singing and stood rooted to the ground, hardly moving. My heart beat so loudly I was sure that everyone else could hear it.

Janet slipped her hand into mine. "This is it," she whispered without moving her head. "If you want to leave, this is the time."

The police took one more step forward and shifted their nightsticks into their right hands. I was panting now—short, sharp, whistling breaths—and I felt light-headed and slightly dizzy. I wondered what it would feel like to have a nightstick hit me on the back of the head. I looked at Charlayne. She was standing tall, looking directly in front of her. I wanted to be like her. I wanted to be strong.

"I'm staying," I whispered.

"We are about to clear this area. Those of you who remain should be prepared to be arrested."

From across the street, the crowd cheered.

I glanced quickly around me. Only a handful of people were left. Some old people. Some young people. Some white. Some black. And off to the side, a Negro minister, a white minister, and with them, unmistakably, was Rabbi Dressler, looking fragile and wearing his *yarmulke*. He and the two ministers were holding hands, quietly singing, "We Shall Overcome."

The police broke from their line and began moving toward us in increasingly rapid steps. They seemed to be coming from all directions.

"Look out!" Janet shouted. "Watch it!"

Someone pushed me and suddenly I was knocked to the pavement. My eyes closed and I felt a sharp pain in my wrist and a stinging sensation in my leg. I was dizzy and confused. I thought, Open your eyes, Betsy. Open your eyes for a minute or two. See if you're okay. But I was too scared to do it. Open your eyes, I shouted to myself. I dared to do it and saw that I was scraped and bleeding but otherwise all right.

I picked myself up and looked around. I couldn't see Janet or Frieda, but Charlayne was over by the police wagon yelling something.

"Fair housing now! Fair housing now! Fair housing now!" she shouted from a distance at the police. I hurried over to join her. The police were paying no attention. They were busy using their nightsticks to shove people into the back of the police wagon.

"Betsy! Are you okay?" Charlayne asked when she saw me.

"Yes," I answered, "just scraped."

"Good! Fair housing now! Fair housing now!" She went back to shouting and I joined in.

From out of nowhere a policeman appeared. "Okay, nigger," he said to Charlayne, or was it Negro? I wasn't sure. "Let's go." He grabbed Charlayne by the arm and forced her toward the police wagon.

"Charlayne!" I screamed. I grabbed her by the other arm and

tugged and struggled in the opposite direction. "Let go of her. Let go!"

"Look at the white nigger. Look at the white nigger. She wants to get arrested!" voices called out, and I knew they were talking about me.

"Let her go! Let her go—please!" I cried out desperately to the policeman.

His only answer was to throw his shoulder against my chest. All my breath left my body and I was hurled backward into the arms of a woman standing nearby.

"Are you all right?" the woman asked.

"Yes," I tried to say, but there was not enough air in my lungs to say it, so all that came out was a wheezing sound. I righted myself just in time to see Charlayne's body collapse and go limp. "Charlayne!" I rasped. "Charlayne!" I yelled, finally mustering enough air to cry out to her.

She didn't answer. The police officer dragged her, like a broken doll, to the police van.

"Charlayne!" I screamed, and despite my fear of the officer, I moved closer. I was not more than two feet away from her. Her body appeared heavy as she was dragged. Her eyes were closed and her face looked almost peaceful.

"Charlayne!" I sobbed. She was conconscious!

Then, miraculously, she turned her face ever so slightly toward me, opened one eye and then closed it rapidly in a wink, and suddenly I remembered something. Passive resistance. Nonviolence. You go limp so it's hard to drag you but they don't have an excuse to beat you up. In my head, Charlayne was explaining, reassuring me. I felt like shouting out loud with joy. Charlayne was okay. She was more than okay. She was a fighter to the end.

The police officer scooped her up and loaded her into the van.

"Fair housing! Fair housing! Fair housing!" I yelled, wishing with everything that was in me that he'd take me, too. Suddenly I wanted to be arrested. More than anything I wanted to be with Charlayne. "Fair housing! Fair housing!" I screamed. But the police officer reached past me into the crowd and grabbed a small Negro man who was just standing there watching. He shoved him in and then climbed into the back of the van and pulled the heavy doors shut.

"Let me in!" I shouted. My hands were tight little fists and they beat over and over, over and over again on the back of the doors. "Let me in!" I was sobbing now, overcome with feelings of helplessness and anger and frustration. "Take me, too!" I cried. "Please!" But they had started the motor up. I could feel the metal trembling under my fingertips.

The police van was pulling away. I held on as tight as I could to the bumper guard. The van lurched forward and my body extended out flat. My feet dragged behind me, scraping slowly and then more rapidly along the street tar.

"Look out!" someone yelled.

"She's going to get hurt!"

It felt like I was being pulled apart. Suddenly the van stopped. My hands slipped off the bumper and the back doors opened, nearly slamming me in the face. A thick blue-clad arm reached out and grabbed me. "Okay, miss," the police officer said, "you're under arrest." He hauled me into the semidarkness of the wagon.

In the light of a single low-watt bulb, I saw two rows of people sitting on two narrow benches, and off in a corner, hunched over and handcuffed, was Charlayne.

"Betsy!" she cried out to me.

"Charlie!" I yelled, but then the van started up and I was thrown against the floor.

I stayed there, aching and scared. I had gotten what I wanted and now I was more frightened then I'd ever been in my life.

13

I looked around the small, khaki-colored room of the precinct house. It was windowless and had no apparent exit other than a door made of heavy iron bars that led down a narrow hallway to some prison cells. The place was in chaos. Demonstrators, some in handcuffs, argued with policemen. Others sang: "I ain't scared of your jail 'cause I want my freedom, I want my freedom, I want my freedom. I ain't scared of your jail 'cause I want my freedom, I want my freedom *now!*" ©

"Come on." The same policeman who had hauled Charlayne and me into the police van pushed us through the crowd and into a long, crooked line of people. At the end of the line was a heavy metal desk and behind it a man who seemed to be the sergeant or chief officer. He waved his arms and shouted angrily at someone in the line. Next to him, another officer held a clipboard in his hands and took down information.

"Name?" he called out.

"What's he taking down names for?" I asked Charlayne. We were handcuffed together and I held Charlayne's hand tightly in mine. "What's he doing?"

"Booking people," she answered nervously.

"You mean . . ."—I had to catch my breath to continue—"after that, you're put in jail?"

"I think so."

I looked again at the door with the bars on it and my legs felt suddenly weak.

I couldn't believe it. I was going to jail. I felt a lump in my chest and before I could stop it, I was crying quietly to myself. Luckily, Charlayne was too busy singing to notice. She had joined in the demonstrators' song and was singing defiantly, "Ain't-a scared of your jails 'cause I want my freedom," © at our policeman.

He just stood there, ignoring her, looking toward the sergeant at the front of the line. I closed my eyes to keep the tears from slipping down my face and saw my mother and father watching television, the red maple outside my bedroom window, Jeannie covered with spaghetti sauce, and a brown wood music box someone had given me. How long would it be before I could see the people and the things I cared about again?

"Betsy!" It was Frieda. I opened my eyes. She was standing next to me, her voice soothing, like a warm summer breeze. "It's okay. It will all be okay. Really it will." I looked up at her. She, too, was crying. Janet, at her side, leaned over and pressed her face, cool and soft and also wet with tears, against mine and then against Charlayne's.

"Well," Frieda said quickly as if she were suddenly disciplining herself. "Let's not just stand here and sulk. Let's see what we can do. Who's in charge?" She spoke loudly to our police officer.

"Ma'am?" the policeman said.

"I asked, who's in charge here?" She stood very tall and looked him straight in the eye. "I am counsel to these children."

Children? I thought. Charlayne and I weren't children. But then I realized Janet's mother wasn't just speaking words. She was choosing special ones very carefully.

"I'm the arresting officer," he answered.

"Have they been charged?" Mrs. Bloom asked.

"Not yet, ma'am, but they will be, as soon as we reach the head of the line and I get my turn with the sergeant." He nodded in the direction of the man at the desk, and as he did so, the line moved forward one place and we were all crushed one step closer together.

"What's the charge?" Mrs. Bloom asked.

"Disorderly conduct," the policeman replied.

"We'll see about that," Frieda said under her breath.

"Excuse me?" the police officer asked.

"Never mind."

"Fred!" A young man wearing a business suit emerged from the crowd and grabbed Mrs. Bloom's arm.

"John!" Frieda spun around. "Who're you here for?"

"Anyone who needs me. The NAACP sent down a carload of us. Dan Kaplan's somewhere in the crowd. So's Jeff DiJoseph and a few of the others. This is quite a mess, isn't it?"

"It sure is," Frieda answered.

"You acting on your own today?"

Mrs. Bloom nodded.

"Well, good luck."

"Thanks, John. You, too."

They smiled at each other and then the young man disappeared into the crowd.

Mrs. Bloom turned back to the officer at Charlayne's side. "Why the handcuffs?"

"Just a precaution," the officer answered. "Just look at this one," he said, indicating Charlayne. Her back was arched, her head thrust forward as if she were challenging the police officer. "And *this* one," he said, pointing to me, "she's *crazy*. She was begging to be arrested."

Frieda said nothing. The line moved forward again and we were all pressed even tighter together.

She tapped us on the shoulder. "I need to ask you a few questions. In private," she added, for the benefit of the policeman.

He shrugged, looking around him. There wasn't much of a chance for privacy with everyone crowded together like so many hornets around a hive.

"How old are you?" Mrs. Bloom spoke to both of us in a quiet, businesslike manner.

Janet leaned forward to listen.

"Sixteen," we answered.

"Both of you? You're exaggerating, aren't you, or have you had your sixteenth birthdays already?"

Charlayne and I nodded.

Mrs. Bloom looked disappointed. "Ever been arrested before?"

"No," I breathed. Even though it was true, there was something about the way Mrs. Bloom was questioning us that made me feel as if I were a criminal or lying.

"How 'bout you, Charlayne?"

Charlayne glanced nervously at me. "Down south. Almost. But, no. Never. This is the first time." She looked both scared and excited.

"Charlayne—father and mother's occupation?"

"Occupation? My father works in a warehouse, my mother in a store."

"Betsy?"

"My dad works for a textile corporation. My mom—well—she doesn't like to say it but she's a housewife."

"Fine," Mrs. Bloom answered. "And you each have one sister, right?"

"Yes," we answered.

"Good. Do well in school?" Mrs. Bloom asked.

"Yeah, sure," Charlayne blushed. "I'm getting an 'A' in Spanish and one in English. The rest I'm not as sure—"

"Good," Mrs. Bloom interrupted. "Betsy?"

"Well, I'm not sure what I'm getting, but I—"

"Good, another 'A' student," Frieda said, interrupting again.

"Next!" a voice boomed. From behind the big desk, the sergeant leaned over and pointed at Charlayne and me and the police officer.

"Name?" the other officer called out.

101

"Charlibethperrybergman," we answered on top of one another.

"One at a time," he yelled.

"Elizabeth Ann Bergman," I said.

"Bergman, Elizabeth," the officer mumbled, writing on his pad. "And you?"

"Charlayne Perry."

"Perry, Charlayne."

"Age?"

"Sixteen," we both answered.

The police officer and the man behind the desk were mumbling something to each other when suddenly Mrs. Bloom slapped her hand down hard on the desk. All three officers stopped what they were doing and looked up.

"How do you do? Frieda Bloom. I'm counsel to these children."

"Children?" the sergeant said. "They're sixteen."

"Barely. What are the charges?"

"Disorderly conduct," the sergeant answered.

"Ridiculous!" Mrs. Bloom announced, startling all of them. "Charge these children and you are violating their rights to freedom of speech and expression as guaranteed by the First and Fourteenth Amendments to the United States Constitution."

A look of extreme annoyance passed over the sergeant's face. "Hold it just a minute, Larry," he said quietly to the policeman with the clipboard. "We got a legal type here and I have to straighten her out."

Mrs. Bloom pretended not to hear. "Charlayne Perry and Elizabeth Bergman, barely sixteen, eldest daughters of hardworking parents, have the constitutional right to express their views," she said firmly.

"That, Mrs. Blum, isn't the issue, and you know it. They were disturbing the peace."

"It's *Bloom*, not Blum," Janet's mother corrected him. "B-L-O-O-M. And they were *not* disturbing the peace."

The sergeant seemed suddenly very tired. "Look, Mrs.

Bloom," he said, pronouncing her name carefully. "I have a lot of people here. I haven't got time for this sort of thing."

"Haven't got time? Well, I assure you these 'A' students haven't got time to go to jail. As for disorderly conduct, it is my understanding that there was a counterdemonstration today, am I right?"

"Yes, but—"

"It seems to me that the people who participated today in the counterdemonstration were congregating in the street, were they not?"

"Well, as a matter of fact—"

"They were obstructing vehicular traffic, were they not?"

"Well, yes, but—"

"And it seems to me they were heckling?"

The sergeant merely nodded.

"As I see it—and I think you will agree with me—my clients, Elizabeth Bergman and Charlayne Perry, along with a number of other concerned citizens, were participating today in an orderly demonstration to express their opinions and rights. If anyone should be charged for disorderly counduct, it seems to me it should be those who congregated in the middle of the street obstructing traffic and heckling. Charging my clients would be a clearcut violation of their constitutional rights—in short, an *unlawful* charge. You wouldn't want to be responsible for that, would you?"

The sergeant waved his hand back and forth in the air. It looked as if he were fanning himself. "Okay, okay, Mrs. Bloom. Your clients are free to go. *Please,"* he said, and there was pleading in his voice, "go."

"*Next,"* the officer with the clipboard called out.

"Wow!" I yelled, and then slammed my hand over my mouth. "Incredible," I whispered to Janet. I was filled with admiration for her mother.

"Yeah, she's good," Janet said quietly, looking at her mother. "The best. That's why I don't want to try to follow in her footsteps. I want to do something of my own."

The police officer took out a key and unlocked our hand-cuffs.

"Thank you. Thank you!" I nearly shouted to Mrs. Bloom.

"Thanks, Mrs. Bloom—Frieda," Charlayne said, and her features filled out and softened so that suddenly I could see just how scared she'd been. "Thanks a lot."

Janet's mother flushed with pleasure, but all she said was, "Don't worry about it. I'm glad I could help out."

The four of us pushed our way to a tiny spot at the side of the room and hugged each other.

"Let's go celebrate!" I yelled. "At the Newport Creamery. I'll pay!" I felt so full of relief, happiness, and pride, it was spilling out of me.

"Not me. At least, not yet," Mrs. Bloom said, smiling. "I can't leave now. I want to join John Mulford and the others and see if I can get a few more people out of this mess. But you girls go ahead. Buy an *Evening Bulletin* for me," she said, freeing herself from our embrace and shoving off back in the direction of the sergeant's desk. "Maybe they had time to squeeze us in before the evening deadline. I want to see what they said. See you later," Frieda said, and was immediately erased from our sight by the crowd.

"She's something," Charlayne said, and Janet nodded, but I barely saw them. The room had misted over. I pushed my way through and saw that I had stepped outside myself and was standing, all dressed up, in front of twelve people in two neat rows. A woman sat high up on a sort of throne nearby watching me. I was waving my arms and speaking passionately to the two rows of people the way I had that day at the PROJECT meeting, and they were listening with all of their attention. I picked up a heavy book, opened it, pointed to a passage, and then spoke some more. I strained to hear what it was that I was saying, but I couldn't make it out. I looked more closely at the book I was holding and saw that it was a lawbook and that the twelve people were a jury. The woman in the box was Frieda Bloom, dressed as a judge.

A sudden warm, dizzying feeling surged through me. It was part excitement, part shock, part fear, part elation. The mist cleared away and I was back in the precinct house with Janet and Charlayne and all the other people.

"Are you okay, Betsy?" Janet asked.

"Yes. Yes! I'm fine. I'm going to be a lawyer," I heard myself say, and the feeling became even more intense. "It's true. It's really true. I'm going to be a lawyer!" It seemed perfectly logical, perfectly right. I felt like flying. "Janet! Charlayne! I've decided. I'm going to be a lawyer!"

"Better you than me," Janet smiled.

"You better be a rich lawyer," Charlayne said.

"Why?"

"She's already forgotten," Charlayne said to Janet. "You promised to take us to the Creamery."

"You're right," I laughed. "But first I have to find a phone booth to call my mother and tell her I'm okay. Then let's get out of this awful place."

Fifteen minutes later, we sat squeezed together at the counter, trying to sip and gulp our way through three Awful Awfuls. Janet unfolded a newspaper and we stared at the headline on the front page of the *Evening Bulletin*. "Trouble at Housing Demo," it read.

"It says the police estimate that there were five hundred demonstrators and two hundred counterdemonstrators. Did you think there were that many people?" Janet asked.

"Nope. I thought it was the other way around," Charlayne answered. "Five hundred of them, two hundred of us."

"You're wrong, Charlayne," I said. "And so is the newspaper. All together there were maybe two hundred and fifty people. A hundred and fifty of us, a hundred of them."

"Well, I'm glad we all agree," Janet said. "Listen to this. It says we started the trouble by calling them names."

"But that's not true!" I shouted. I was outraged. How could a newspaper make a mistake? "What's the matter with this paper?

I thought it was supposed to report the *facts*. There were reporters there with press badges and everything. You'd think they'd get things right. You'd think at least they could count. And if they can't count, they can at least hear. If they listened, they'd have heard that we didn't start it, and then you'd think that—" I stopped shouting. Charlayne and Janet were laughing, and across the counter serveral people had paused in the middle of their sundaes and were staring at me. "What's so funny?" I asked.

"You," Charlayne said. "You're gonna be some lawyer! A regular locomotive!"

"I'm sorry," I said. "I got carried away."

"So what?" Janet said.

"Yeah," Charlayne added. "So what?"

Yeah, I thought. So what?

"I'm also pretty naïve, I guess. About the newspaper and all."

"So what?" Janet said.

"Yeah," Charlayne added. "So what?"

Yeah, I thought. So what?

Janet and Charlayne were smiling at me over their Awful Awfuls and I felt wonderful. Simply wonderful. Here were these two people who accepted and liked me for what I was. I clenched my hands into fists and began pounding them up and down, up and down on the counter.

"What are you doing?" Charlayne and Janet asked, glancing nervously around the ice-cream parlor. Absolutely everyone was staring at me, and the manager was coming over.

"Who am I?" I shouted to Janet and Charlayne, not caring.

"What do you mean?" Janet asked.

"Who am I?" I repeated.

"I don't know. Who are you?" Charlayne asked.

"Don't you know?"

"No!" they shouted.

"A counter demonstrator!" I giggled.

Charlayne and Janet roared with laughter. "You're a crazy person, Betsy," Janet said between laughs.

"*Es loca,*" Charlayne said. "*Es* truly *loca.*"

They were teasing me—something they'd never done before. So much had happened among us. Now I knew for sure that we were friends. Good friends.

14

It was an unusually warm Saturday morning in early spring and I awoke feeling depressed. It wasn't anything I could put my finger on. No thoughts. Just a vague emptiness in the place in my chest where my heart was supposed to be. I threw on an old shirt and a pair of jeans and dragged myself downstairs.

"What's the matter?" my father asked as I opened one of the kitchen cabinets and stared blankly into it.

I shrugged, and pulled out a box of Cocoa Puffs, a box of Sugar Pops, and a box of Trix.

"Something bothering you?"

I looked up and stared at my father. He sat by himself at the kitchen table holding a mug of coffee, a bialy, and the newspaper. It was get-your-own-breakfast day and the only day when my mother wasn't after him to "eat properly."

"Betsy!" he said with annoyance when I didn't answer.

"Yeah?" I set the boxes on the table and reached for some milk and a bowl.

"Are you going to answer me or not? What *is* it?"

"Nothing," I said. "I guess it's just one of those days, you know? When you feel blah."

My father stared at me, opened his mouth to speak, and then

closed it again. Fortunately for me, he had decided to say no more.

"Hello, you guys," Jeannie yelled. She bounced into the kitchen and began preparations for a plate of spaghetti. "How's it going?"

"Except for the fact that I have to work today, *I* feel wonderful," my dad answered. "But Betsy is another story. She feels 'blah.' "

"Oh, yeah? What's up, Bets?"

"Nothing," I answered, wishing they'd both leave me alone. I poured some Puffs, Pops, and Trix into a bowl and added a couple of spoonfuls of sugar.

"Yuk!" Jeannie said, watching me. "You're not feeling suicidal, are you? How can you eat that junk?"

"Just mind your own spaghetti," I answered.

For once Jeannie listened and turned away. "Where's mom?" she asked my father.

"Here I am," my mother answered. She stood at the door to the kitchen holding the mail and waving an opened letter in her hand as if to fan herself. She seemed tremendously excited. "I'm unstuck, Ted!" she called to my father.

"What, Barbara?" my father asked, looking concerned.

"I'm unstuck!" she repeated, laughing. "Ask Betsy. She knows what I mean."

"I do?"

"Yes! They admitted me to Pembroke as a sophomore."

"No kidding!" My father jumped up and threw his arms around her.

Jeannie danced around the kitchen.

"Oh, mom!" I said, remembering our conversation and suddenly realizing what "unstuck" meant.

"I did it, Betsy—finally. Thanks to you."

"To me? What did I do?"

"It was our talk. It gave me courage and I went back in again to see the admissions officer."

"But why didn't you tell us?" my father asked.

"Because all the other times I talked and did nothing. This time, no talk. Action. That's what I kept saying over and over again to myself. No talk. Action. And it worked!" My mother's face was bright with pleasure.

"Momma, that's wonderful," I said quietly to her.

"It is," she said shyly. "Do I look like a college student?" She fluffed up her hair. "I'll be the oldest student there. What will everyone think?"

"They'll love you," my father said.

"I'm not sure. I'm not sure I can do it. I'm nervous."

"I'll help you, mom," I said. "I'll help you be brave."

"Oh, Betsy!" My mother's eyes grew wet and a small tear blossomed in the corner of one eye and slipped slowly down her cheek. "Thanks," she said, and hugged me. Then she straightened up and tried to hide her emotion. "What's everyone eating today?"

"Sugar and starch," my father answered, looking at me and then at Jeannie.

"And caffeine," my mother said, eyeing his coffee cup.

"When she starts yelling at me, it's time to go to work," my father announced, winking at her. "How 'bout a family celebration tonight? Dinner at Camille's Roman Garden. Okay?"

Jeannie squealed and my mother nodded and smiled a special smile at him.

"See you ladies tonight," my father said, grabbing his coat and giving us each a kiss.

"See you," Jeannie called to him.

I just nodded. My mother left to walk him out the door and I picked up my spoon and chased a Sugar Pop around my bowl. My depression had lifted for a minute or two, but now it was back again.

Jeannie forked some spaghetti onto a plate and sat down across from me at the table. "What's eating you?" she asked.

"You," I snapped.

She leaned her head over her plate and poked at the mound of spaghetti with her fingers.

"Sorry," I said miserably.

Jeannie didn't answer.

"I'm in a crummy mood. I didn't mean to bite your head off. You want to do something today?"

"Can't. I'm going bowling with Iris and Wendy. Want to come?"

Bowling with Jeannie's friends. As if I didn't have any friends of my own. The thought sent me even deeper into depression. "Nope," I answered, finally realizing what was bothering me. I was lonely. It was as simple as that. And now I had an idea. "What's the temperature?" I asked.

Jeannie got up and went to the window to check the thermometer. "Wow!" she exclaimed. "Eight-thirty and already sixty-five degrees."

"Think I'll call Charlie," I said, immediately feeling better. I picked up the receiver and dialed her number.

"Hello?" Charlayne answered after only one ring.

"It's me," I said. "Eight-thirty a.m. and already sixty-five degrees Fahrenheit. Want to go to Newport for the day? I'll see if I can get the car."

"Oh, Betsy, I *caaan't,*" Charlayne said, leaning on the last word. "I have to take Pauline to the dentist today. She has an appointment."

Suddenly my depression was back. "Oh, well—another time," I said casually, as if it really didn't matter. "Gotta go. My mom needs the phone," I lied, rushing to hang up and hide my overblown emotions. What was the *matter* with me today? Why was I so upset? Going off to Newport wasn't all that important. But maybe it was—because it took me less than thirty seconds to dial Janet's number.

"Hello," a drowsy voice answered.

"Were you sleeping?" I asked.

"You want the truth?"

"I guess not." I took a deep breath to expel some of the nervousness I felt. "Look out the window. It's a beautiful day. Come to Newport with me. I'll drive."

"Aw, Betsy. I can't. My aunt is here from New York to spend the weekend."

111

"Okay," I said, feeling like I was drowning, and worrying that I might embarrass myself by crying. "Forget it."

"You want to come over and meet my aunt?" Janet offered, hearing my disappointment.

"No offense, but, no. . . . And anyway, it was just an idea. Gotto go."

"Okay. See you," Janet said.

"Yeah. Bye." I slammed the phone down and slumped into my chair.

"Janet's busy," my mother said. At some point she had come into the room and had been watching me.

"Yeah. Charlayne, too." With the back of my spoon, I flattened a Sugar Pop against the side of the bowl. Then I watched as it sank slowly into the graying milk.

"So what are you going to do today?" my mother asked.

"Nothing," I answered. "Nothing." All of a sudden I liked that word. It seemed to express a whole lot. "Guess I'll do noth-thing," I repeated, pronouncing the word carefully.

"I told her she could come bowling with me," Jeannie said, her mouth stuffed with spaghetti, "but she didn't want to."

Jeannie was getting on my nerves again, but when I looked up I saw that she was staring at me with concern. For a kid sister, she was really pretty considerate.

"Don't worry about me," I said to her. "I'll be okay. I'm just having a bad day."

"Betsy, sweetheart," my mother said, coming over and putting her arms around me. "What's the matter?"

There was something about the way she called me sweetheart, something about the way she held me close to her, that made me feel, all of a sudden, the way I had when I was a baby nestling in her arms.

"Nothing's the matter," I said, fighting back tears. I wanted to be grown up. I didn't want my mother to see the baby in me. And I certainly didn't want Jeannie to see it.

"Jeannie," my mother called as if reading my mind.

Jeannie nodded obediently, picked up her bowl of spaghetti, and left the room.

"Now, what is it, baby?" my mother asked. She pushed a strand of hair away from my face.

The dam burst and I started to cry. "I don't know. I don't know *why*, but I feel empty . . . lonely."

My mother was silent for a moment. "You know, Betsy, that I try not to intrude in your affairs, but I haven't been able to keep from noticing that you've cut yourself off from some of the things that used to be so important to you. Like PROJECT meetings. You never go anymore. Do you think that's such a good idea?"

"I told you about those people. They're hypocrites."

"All of them, Betsy?"

"No, but a lot of them."

"What you really mean is Bernie. She let you down in some way, didn't she?"

I didn't answer. But I felt chilled and frightened, as if I had just slipped off a rock into some cold, dark water.

"You used to be such good friends. I still don't really understand what happened between you two, but I think it's been left long enough. It's time you called her."

Again I didn't answer.

"Betsy?"

"Forget it," I said.

My mother kissed the side of my head. Her lips felt soft and light like butterfly wings. "Oh, Betsy. You've taught me so much about courage. Now *you* have to be brave. Call Bernie and see if you can talk it out."

I looked up at my mother. She was smiling at me and her eyes gleamed with a strength I had never seen before. My mother was finally behind me, pushing me and urging me to do something I was afraid to do. I leaned my head against her chest. I could hear her heart beating.

"Okay, momma," I whispered. "I'll call Bernie."

15

I didn't ring the bell, beep the horn, or go in to get her, I just waited in the Rambler with the motor on for Bernie to come out of her house. Every once in a while I tapped my foot on the accelerator and filled the air with exhaust fumes. I guess I needed to feel powerful.

After about five minutes, Bernie appeared, neatly dressed in a round-collared blouse, a yellow cardigan sweater, and madras bermudas. It was Bernie, all right, but somehow, in some as yet unidentifiable way, she looked different to me. Less spunky? More serious? I wasn't sure. She carried a large beach bag. Out of the top of it I could see Itzhak's heart-shaped head peering out.

"Hi," Bernie said softly as she got in and closed the door.

"Hi," I said.

I pulled the car out of park and started down the street. Neither of us spoke. It was obvious that I had called Bernie to have things out with her, to talk finally about all the things that had happened between us, but now I felt too nervous to do it. My mind was blank and I couldn't think of a single thing to say.

Why in the world had I let myself get into such a situation? I wondered. Here we were about to be cooped up in a tiny space for approximately one hour, about to spend an entire day together, and we couldn't even make small talk. The silence was painful. Even so, neither of us had the courage to break it.

"Thought Itzhak could use a day at the beach," Bernie said finally. "It's been an awfully cold winter."

"Right," I said, wondering if she was referring to the weather or to us.

"Betsy?"

"What?" I felt like a mountain climber preparing to take a step across a ravine. I didn't dare look at her. Instead, I pretended to be absorbed in my driving.

Bernie didn't answer.

"Did you say something?" I asked, intensely studying the bumper of the car in front of us.

"No," she answered quickly. "I mean I—never mind."

I leaned forward and turned on the radio. "Again yesterday," a smooth-voiced announcer said, "in the city of Birmingham, Alabama, Martin Luther King led hundreds of demonstrators in protest against what has been termed 'the capital of segregation.' Police under the direction of Eugene 'Bull' Connor, commissioner of public safety, used police dogs and fire hoses to subdue the demonstrators, many of whom were Negro youngsters under eighteen. More than one hundred people were injured. Fifty people were arrested. Demonstrations are scheduled to continue again today."

I was holding my head so still and keeping my eyes so straight ahead that my neck muscles had begun to vibrate. Somehow the last thing we needed was to hear the latest civil-rights news. I pushed the button and switched the station. Peter, Paul and Mary's homogeneous voices sang out, and soon Itzhak, curled in Bernie's lap, joined in.

> Puff the magic dragon
> [Ayow ayow yow]
> Lived by the sea
> And frolicked [ayow ayow] in the autumn mist
> In a land called Honah–Lee.

I stole a glance at Bernie and started to grin. Bernie grinned back and we broke into a song of relief: "Ayow ayow a yowa, Ayow yow yow yow yow . . ."

Itzhak was howling now that he had a couple of cronies to sing with. Together we sounded like three old drunks.

"The latest singing sensation," Bernie giggled. "Betsy and Bernie and the One and Only Hepcat."

"Right," I said, and immediately stopped singing. For a minute or two, I had relaxed, but now I was tense again. My old last name was back. For the last few months, I'd been Betsy by herself. Betsy Bergman. It had been a little bit lonely but otherwise nice.

"What's the matter?" Bernie asked. "What did I say?"

"Nothing." How could I possibly explain? "Nothing."

We were silent again, passing through Barrington. As we approached Bristol, the breeze carried with it the fresh tangy smell of sand and salt water. The world felt sleepy and sloweddown. Ahead of us a roadside stand announced that it sold "Tasty Fried Clams" and I stepped on the brake and pulled into the parking area. "Come on," I called to Bernie, jumping out of the car.

Bernie grabbed Itzhak and followed.

"Two orders of fried clams, two Cokes, and a large order of onion rings," I told the guy at the window.

"Make that just one order of clams. I'll take a fish sandwich instead," Bernie said.

"You aren't suddenly keeping kosher, are you?" I laughed. It felt good to joke with Bernie again.

"Yes," Bernie said shyly. "I am."

"You're kidding! No more shrimp with lobster sauce? No more bacon and eggs?"

Bernie nodded.

"Wow!" I didn't know what to say, so I just handed Bernie her fish sandwich and reached for the carton of clams. I popped a clam into my mouth and chewed through the rich batter to the sweet rubber strip underneath. "These are great. Are you sure you don't want one?" I asked. I felt guilty for tempting her, but I also missed the old times. I wanted Bernie to share with me the way she used to.

Bernie shook her head.

"You can still eat onion rings, can't you?"

"Sure." She grabbed a handful and stuffed them into her mouth.

Itzhak rubbed his side against my leg and I leaned over to feed him a clam. "He isn't keeping kosher now, is he?"

Bernie paused for a moment. "Yes, he is," she said quietly. "I'll give him some of my fish." She broke off a piece, let Itzhak sniff it, and then put it down next to him on the pavement.

"You've changed," I said. "The minute I saw you, I thought you looked somehow different."

Bernie nodded. "You, too."

"How can you tell?"

"I don't know, but I can."

I shrugged, uncomfortable. "Let's go. We can eat the rest of this junk on the road."

We got back into the car and drove the rest of the way to Newport in silence.

"Have you got any money? Do you want to tour one of the mansions? The Breakers is open," I said when we got there.

"No," Bernie said, "let's just walk along Cliff Walk."

"You sure?" I asked, nervous. I wanted to tour the Vanderbilt mansion or something. Have them tell us all about the Italian marble and the fancy antique furniture. That way I wouldn't have to talk. I wouldn't have to deal with all the painful silences between us.

"I'm sure," Bernie said. "They wouldn't let Itzhak in anyway and I'd hate to leave him in the car. Besides . . . we have to . . ."

"I know," I sighed, "talk about things."

Bernie nodded.

"Okay." I said nervously, getting out of the car.

We walked along the high narrow path that followed the shoreline and passed in front of some of the elegant old Newport mansions. It was a magnificent day. The ocean licked and slapped at the beach below us and the sun burned round in the sky, depositing thousands of tiny rippling diamonds in the water. Far out on the horizon, fishing boats bobbed up and down. Overhead the gulls squabbled and squawked, and ahead of us Itzhak prowled and stalked. The world smelled of fish and he was vigilant and ready.

"Well?" Bernie said.

"Well, what?" I asked, in a last-ditch attempt to avoid the inevitable.

"Come *on*, you *know*," Bernie said impatiently. "Begin."

I glanced over the steep cliff down to the water below and recalled the image I had had of the climber at the edge of a ravine. I saw him lift his foot in the air above the ravine . . . "Just answer one question for me," I said, "just one question."

"Okay."

"How come you tried to stop me from speaking out?"

Bernie didn't answer. For a long while, she walked along close beside me, staring at the path in front of us, saying nothing. When she finally raised her eyes, they were wet with tears. "I don't exactly know," she said. "I've asked myself that question over and over and I'm not sure I know the answer yet. I've thought a lot about that day and tried to figure out what happened between us and what led up to it. One thing that keeps coming back to me is your saying you thought I was brave."

"Yeah," I interrupted, starting to cry. "I thought you were. I did. I thought I could look up to you. You weren't just my friend, you were my teacher. But you let me down, Bernie. How come? How come, Bernie?" I was crying hard now. There was no way to hide it.

"But, Betsy, I was never the brave one. You were."

"Oh, come on," I said. "You know I've always been scared to do everything. You even called me a northern fried chicken. Now you're just trying to take it back."

"I remember when I called you a northern fried chicken. It was the day we collected food. I looked out the car window and saw Charlayne standing there with her sign on and I thought, this isn't just the two of us and an afternoon at the supermarket, this is for real. And for a minute or two, I was really scared, and then before I knew what was happening, we were fighting."

"You were scared, Bernie? I can't believe that. It didn't seem that way."

"Maybe not. But I was—at least at first. I told you once before that I don't think a whole lot about things the way you do. I've realized lately that not thinking about things made me careless, but it also made it easier for me to do them. You're the opposite of me. You think a lot, sometimes too much, so you're more aware of how things can go wrong. That makes everything scarier for you, but in the end you're the one who manages to overcome your fear and do what has to be done." Bernie stopped walking and looked at me. "It's true, Betsy."

I felt confused. My mother had said the same thing to me. Could it be true.

"But, Bernie, you still haven't told me why you tried to stop me from speaking at the meeting."

"I already told you, Betsy. I don't know. It was a lot of things, I guess. Me and my parents mostly. I've been thinking so much about them and me. I told you I realized I've been careless. I've never really thought seriously about myself or anything. All I've ever done is react to my parents. When they've come down hard on me, I've done some stupid, kidlike, rebellious thing like run off with a guy from Brown. When I want to stay on their good side, I try to please them by being just like them. Then there's me, caught in the middle, wondering who I really am— their black sheep or their goody-two-shoes.

"When you stood up in that Meeting Hall to shout out what you felt, what you believed, you were incredibly brave and it scared me to death. I was trying then, so hard, to be their good little girl. And there was my best friend, doing something hard, shouting out who she was and what she believed in while sitting next to her was scared little me wanting it all to be just a party so I wouldn't have to think about anything, wouldn't have to figure out who I was. With every word that came out of your mouth, I knew I was losing you and your friendship, that we were getting farther and farther apart. You, knowing all about yourself, and me, knowing nothing about myself.

"I wanted to have a party and not dance. I thought about that a lot. Having a party and not dancing. It seemed to sum up what was wrong with me. So I decided to find out what works for me, what's mine. I have to be brave enough to dance the way you do. Do you know what I mean, Betsy? Do you?"

"I think so," I answered.

Bernie was crying hard now. Her tears slipped down her face one right after another and were carried away by the sea breeze. I put my arms around her and we hugged each other and cried together. Itzhak curled around our legs, trying to offer some comfort.

"But, Bernie, I'm not brave. Really, I'm not. I was even too chicken to talk this out with you. I—"

"Who called whom?" Bernie asked, using the sleeve of her sweater to mop her face free of tears.

"I called you. But it was my mother who pushed me to do it. She—"

"But you *did* it. Don't you see, Betsy?"

I shook my head. I still didn't see. I still didn't feel brave.

"I've told you before," Bernie said, "you underestimate yourself."

"Maybe . . ." I sat down on a boulder at the edge of the path and looked out across the flat expanse of gray-green ocean. Out near the spot where the sky met the sea, a trawler dragged its nets across the ocean floor pursued by a semicircle of hungry sea gulls. On the beach below us, an old woman held her skirt high and waded in the foam. "Bernie?"

"What?" She sat down beside me.

"How come you're keeping kosher now? It sounds suspicious to me. Too much like your parents. Is it you trying to be good again?"

Bernie picked a piece of gravel from the path and flung it out over the cliff to the rocks below. "I don't think so. Look." She reached into her beach bag, withdrew a color brochure, and handed it to me.

On the brochure was a photo of some girls sitting in squat, silver-green trees. The caption beneath it read, "Harvesting Olives."

"Turn it over," Bernie said.

On the other side, in thick brown lettering, it said, "Life on a Kibbutz: An Adventure in Living."

"What is this, Bernie?" I asked.

Bernie's face flushed the color of sunrise. "It's what I'm going to do, Betsy. In a year. After I graduate."

"Go to Israel and work on a kibbutz?"

Bernie nodded.

"You're kidding! Do your parents know?"

Bernie shook her head. "I'm not telling them until it's all settled. They still want me to do the Pembroke, Jewish-doctor thing, so I'll apply and if Pembroke is dumb enough to admit me, I just won't go."

"But, Bernie, are you sure you're not just rebelling again?"

"I'm sure, Betsy. I want to do something big. Something that's my own. Something for me and for other people, too. Like you."

"Like me?"

"Yes, like when you signed up for that demonstration. . . . You know, you were right about me when you called me a hypocrite. I thought about that, too. And I realized I have a lot to work out. I shouldn't be trying to help Negro people. I'm not comfortable with them. I feel only the things that make them different from me instead of the things that make them the same. I guess I *am* bigoted. Maybe because I've never known anyone Negro. Up close, I mean. Anyway, maybe someday I'll change that. I don't know . . . but in the meantime, I want to help someone, the way you've been doing. I know Hebrew, I know about being Jewish, and I want to start by helping the people in Israel."

"That's great, Bernie." I meant it, but somehow the words sounded flat and empty. Instead of feeling happy for Bernie, I was sad. "Two roads diverged in a yellow wood," I said, quoting a line of a Robert Frost poem.

121

'What are you trying to say?" Bernie asked.

"I'm not sure," I answered. "The words just came into my head. I guess I mean that, in more ways than one, we're off in different directions."

Bernie nodded and clasped my hand.

"I've gotten to know Janet Bloom's mother a bit and I've decided I'm going to be a lawyer, Bernie, like her. A civil-rights lawyer."

"You'll be a good one. You have all the ingredients except for one thing."

"What's that?"

"You're too harsh."

"What do you mean?"

"Why did you stop coming to PROJECT meetings?"

"I don't know. After that meeting, I just felt like you were—like they were all a bunch of hypocrites."

"See what I mean? You're too harsh. They're not *all* hypocrites, and some of them—some of us—are trying."

I felt ashamed. It was another thing my mother had said, and Bernie was right. She raised her eyes and stared out toward the horizon, looking sad.

"What is it, Bernie?"

"Nothing. I was just thinking about Janet Bloom and what you said before about how we're off in different directions. You and Charlayne and Janet are good friends now, aren't you?"

I nodded.

"You know, we had a meeting last month of the PROJECT Nominating Committee. Janet Bloom and I are both on it. I've never cared much for her, but she really isn't so bad. She's just so—well—you know—the opposite of how I've been."

"Committed to things. Serious."

"Yes. In a way, I guess I've always been jealous of her. She always seems to know what she's doing. Somehow I guess I always figured I'd lose you to someone like that. That one day we'd stop being Betsy and Bernie."

Bernie looked at me, her eyes full of tears again.

"It couldn't go on forever that way, Bernie. Sooner or later the day had to come when you had to be Bernie by yourself and I had to be Betsy by myself."

"That day has come, Betsy, hasn't it?" Bernie said quietly.

"Yes," I nodded.

I took Bernie's hand in mine, feeling a vague, longing sadness that must be what people call "nostalgia." Part of me wished I could turn things back to simpler times, to the way things used to be between Bernie and me, but the other part of me knew I couldn't and shouldn't. We both had a lot of things to do and experience on our own and we could only do them by ourselves, without each other.

"We'll still be friends, Betsy, won't we?"

"Of course," I said, but deep inside me a little child who knew the truth was weeping. It would never be the same again and I knew it, the child knew it, and when I looked at Bernie's face, I saw that Bernie knew it, too.

16

"I don't know, Betsy," my mother said as she pulled into a parking spot on Lloyd Avenue. She switched off the motor and used her arm to wipe some perspiration from her forehead.

It was scarcely 5:00 a.m. on an already steamy August morning. Across the street, two yellow school buses glowed in the early-dawn darkness. Outside them, several dozen people stood in small groups waiting to board and make the long trip to Washington, D.C., for a civil-rights demonstration that everyone hoped would be the largest ever held.

"Look, Betsy," my mother said carefully. "I'm trying hard not to let my old fears affect my judgment. Even so, I just don't know. This time it may be too dangerous. I guess what I'm trying to say is—are you sure you should go?"

"Mom," I sighed, taking a deep breath to keep calm. "It'll be okay. You're supposed to be cheering me on, remember? Helping me dare to go farther?"

"I know," she said apologetically. "Still, I *am* your mother and I'm worried. So much has happened lately. And Washington, D.C., is the South. How do you know there won't be trouble?"

"I'm not sure. I just *feel* it. I know I'm right. It's going to be fine."

I didn't know why I wasn't scared this time, but the truth of it was that I wasn't. The news lately had been full of incredible violence, and still I wasn't afraid. In June, President Kennedy had asked Congress to enact a civil-rights bill that would allow Negro people the freedom to use any hotels, restaurants, stores, or theaters that white people used. But so far, the bill hadn't passed and there had been more and more violence. The police were routinely using police dogs and fire hoses to stop demonstrators; the homes of several civil-rights leaders had been bombed, along with a desegregated motel; and, worst of all, Medgar Evers, a civil-rights worker for the National Association for the Advancement of Colored People, had been murdered right in his own driveway. It seemed that with every passing day some new and awful thing was taking place.

I looked out into the darkness and trembled. There were a few white faces but mostly black ones in the gathering crowd. Everyone looked a bit strange, the men and boys in business suits, the women and girls dressed up, and everyone lugging Thermoses, lunch boxes, and brown paper bags. I was wearing my best sleeveless cotton dress and flat shoes for walking. I carried my own paper bag with a bottle of soda and two peanut-butter-and-banana sandwiches in it. We had all been told to "look respectable" and bring food.

"Betsy!" someone called. From out of the shadows, Janet's enthusiastic face appeared and was soon framed by the car window. "Hi, Mrs. Bergman. You coming, too?"

I listened to the dashboard clock ticking out the slow seconds before my mother managed to get out an answer. "No, Janet, I just came to drop Betsy off. I—"

"Oh, come on. It'll be fun," Janet interrupted. She glanced quickly in my direction and blinked ever so slightly; I couldn't be sure if she was winking at me or if I was imagining it.

"Yes, please come. I've been wanting to meet Betsy's mother," another voice piped up, and all of a sudden, there was Frieda's face right beside Janet's. "Frieda Bloom," she announced, and thrust her arm through the window across my chest until her hand met my mother's. "But if you want to get on my good side, you'll call me Fred."

"Barbara Bergman," my mother said nervously, taking Frieda's hand in hers. "I've heard a lot about you."

"Well, are you coming?" Frieda asked, ignoring the pleasantries and getting right back to the point.

I pressed myself against the back of the seat, trying to make my body as flat, invisible, and out-of-the-way as possible. I didn't want any part of this. I'd told Janet a little about my mother's problems, but now that I saw what she and Frieda were up to, it was obvious that I hadn't told her enough.

"No," my mother said with difficulty. "I leave these things to Betsy. I'm not someone who can—what I mean to say is—I can't—"

"Why can't you?" Frieda interrupted, smiling. She looked directly into my mother's eyes in much the same way that Janet often looked into mine.

"Because."

"Yes, why can't you?" I heard myself ask.

My mother just stared at me. Her mouth moved, but no words came out.

"Why can't you?" I repeated.

"Well, for one thing," she finally said, "I didn't bring any food."

"You can have one of my peanut-butter-and-banana sandwiches," I said.

Frieda wrinkled her nose. "Never mind that. You can have one of my chicken sandwiches."

My mother smiled slightly, then took my hand, "Oh, Betsy," she said pleadingly.

"What?"

"I'd have to call dad and tell him."

"So?"

"Do you really think I . . ."

I nodded excitedly.

"Allright," she said, letting out her breath. "I'll go."

I couldn't believe my ears. I leaned across the seat and embraced her, and when I sat up and moved to get out of the car, I saw something unmistakable. Frieda was winking at me.

"Come on," Frieda said. "The old ladies will sit together."

"Okay," my mother agreed. We got out and she locked the car doors behind us.

"Betsy! Janet! Fred!" It was Charlayne's unmistakable voice. She stood across the street next to a Negro girl with a short, lacquered pageboy and waved to us.

"Mom," I said with excitement. "It's Charlie. Come on. I want to introduce you." All of a sudden, I wanted to show off my mother. "Mom," I called, leading my mother over to where Charlayne was standing. "This is Charlayne. Charlayne Perry. Charlie, this is my mother. She's coming with us." I could barely keep my feet still on the pavement. They were dancing underneath me.

"Oh, I'm so glad to meet you," Charlayne said. Her face was warm and shining.

"Likewise." My mother smiled at her.

"This is my friend Ruthie," Charlayne said, "She's coming, too. And this is Betsy. And Mrs. Bergman."

"And Janet." From behind me, Janet stuck her arm through a slot between me and my mother and shook Ruthie's hand.

"And Janet's mother, Frieda," Mrs. Bloom added.

"Hi," Ruthie said, flashing a warm, shy smile. She seemed overwhelmed by all the introductions, and then I remembered that Charlayne had mentioned her name that day in the parking lot at Almacs. Ruthie was the friend who was too scared to come and collect food for Food for Freedom. Suddenly it was all I could do to keep myself from hugging her.

"All aboard the Freedom Express!" someone called up ahead.

My mother hurried into a nearby pay phone to call my father. The bus doors opened and everyone pressed forward. Slowly but surely we climbed onto the bus and set up housekeeping, all of us piling and stuffing our belongings into the overhead racks, making ourselves comfortable. Janet sat next to the window and I sat on the aisle, across the way from Charlayne and Ruthie. In front of Janet and me, my mother joined Frieda, and soon they were deep in conversation.

Before long, and without any fanfare, our bus and the bus behind it shook, chortled, rumbled, and were on their noisy way to Washington, D.C.

I looked out the window past Janet into the early-morning darkness and watched the black-velvet-ribbonlike city streets slowly unravel behind us. Off on the horizon the sky was awakening, blushing pale pink and yellow. A few birds flew, like accent marks, across it. Around me people spoke softly together as if afraid to disturb the dawn. The world felt fresh and new.

"I have something to tell you," Janet whispered. She smiled the smile of someone who knows a secret.

"What?"

Instead of telling me, she leaned over and hugged me.

"What?" I repeated.

"Well," she said slowly, "Kenny Klein graduated in June and so PROJECT is in the market for a new vice-president. Guess who was nominated by the Nominating Committee to be the next vice-president?"

"Who?"

"You!"

"You're kidding, aren't you?" Inside me, everything came to an abrupt halt.

"No! Isn't that wonderful?"

"No," I said, feeling dreadful. "It's terrible."

"What's the matter?" Janet asked.

"How can I run for vice-president? I don't even attend the meetings anymore. You know I haven't been since February when I ran out."

Janet nodded.

"So?" I said.

"So, when you're vice-president, I guess you'll have to make it to the meetings." Janet's face was full of mischief. "They need someone mild-mannered and easygoing like you to goose them the way you did the last time."

I smiled and felt happy that Janet knew me well enough to make fun of me. But then, a moment later, I was filled with sadness and longing.

"What is it?" Janet asked.

"Oh, nothing. I was just wondering about Bernie, wondering what she'd think of this if she knew about it."

"*Think?* She's the one who suggested we nominate you!"

"You're kidding!"

"No. She even told us what you'd say—that you'd give all kinds of reasons as to why you couldn't run, why you *shouldn't* run—but that we should ignore you and make sure that you did."

"She said *that?*"

"Yes, and also something else," Janet said, looking mischievous again. "As I recall, she used the words 'tough customer.' Yes, that was it—that you were a tough customer but the best person for the job."

"She said *that?*" I asked again, tremendously pleased.

Janet grinned at me.

"But, Janet," I said, "you don't know me the way Bernie does. I'd be scared to death to be vice-president."

Janet just nodded. "So?"

"Do it!" Charlayne said. Ruthie smiled shyly.

"Okay," I said, "a little respect for the next vice-president."

Janet, Charlayne, and Ruthie applauded.

"I've got something else to tell you," Janet said with excitement.

"What's that?"

"I'm joining the Peace Corps. I sent for all the information yesterday."

"You did? What did Frieda say?"

Janet smiled. "You mean you haven't heard her bragging? She thinks it's wonderful!"

In front of us, my mother laughed as if she had heard Janet's decision, but then I heard the rustle of whispered words and realized that she hadn't heard anything and was occupied with Fred.

"Wonder what they're talking about?" Janet said.

I shrugged and felt a twinge of jealousy at being excluded. But then I couldn't decide whom I was jealous of—my mother for having Frieda all to herself, or Frieda for having my mother all to herself.

The sun was finally up and the Connecticut Turnpike looked clean and neat in clear, soft light. From the back of the bus, someone began singing one of the recent freedom songs.

> If you miss me at the back of the bus,
> You can't find me nowhere,
> Oh, oh, come on over to the front of the bus,
> I'll be riding up there.
> I'll be riding up there.
> I'll be riding up there.
> Oh, oh, come on over to the front of the bus,
> I'll be riding up there.

Soon we had all joined in, and suddenly the rattling, chugging, creaking old school bus seemed to be sashaying down the highway wearing dancing shoes instead of wheels.

> If you miss me in the cotton fields,
> You can't find me nowhere,
> Oh, oh, come on over to the courthouse,
> I'll be voting right there.
> I'll be voting right there.
> I'll be voting. . . .

My mother stood up, leaned over the back of her seat, and wordlessly kissed me. Then she returned to the singing.

> If you miss me on the picket line,
> You can't find me nowhere,
> Oh, oh, come on over to the city jail,
> I'll be roomin' over there.

I'll be roomin' over there.
I'll be roomin' over there.
Oh, oh, come on over to the city jail,
I'll be roomin' there.©

We sang and talked and napped until we reached the New Jersey Turnpike. Suddenly the world smelled like an egg going bad. The smoke from chemical plants and oil refineries combined with the thick August heat and clung heavily together.

On the side of the turnpike in a worn-out rest-stop area with bathrooms and picnic tables, we stopped for an early lunch. Everyone piled out of the buses and made for a table or a bit of burnt-out grass. Under a wilted tree, we found a spot and unpacked our various lunches. From where I sat, I could watch people here and there as they stretched and set about the motions of feeding themselves and making themselves comfortable.

"Bologna for a tuna sandwich! Bologna for tuna! Anyone want to trade?" a middle-aged woman with skin the color of molasses called out.

"Over here, dear," a cream-faced older woman answered.

Under another tree, a group of young men in black business suits laughed and removed their jackets.

Leaning against the wall of the bathroom building, a young woman nursed her small baby. "Da da da," it gurgled, pulling away from her to look around. "A-dee," it said, and then returned to its lunch.

"Want some chicken?" Charlayne asked. She opened a cake box and revealed a huge golden mound of chicken. "My mama's best," she said in her thickest southern drawl. "Now don't you all be shy."

Frieda helped herself to a drumstick, my mom took a thigh, and soon we were all coated with a smooth, thin layer of salty, delicious grease. Everyone shared everything and before long I was full of chicken, peanut butter, hard-boiled eggs, an apple, some pound cake, and an oatmeal cookie.

"I'm sick," I moaned.

"Me, too," Janet sighed, holding her stomach. "What a feast!"

Charlayne lay back on the grass. "Save me," she groaned sleepily.

Suddenly we heard a strange sound, something like a cheer. We looked over toward the highway.

"Will you *look* at *that!*" Frieda exclaimed.

"There must be twenty of them," my mother said with surprise.

"More," Charlayne said, standing up.

Streaming down the turnpike was bus after bus carrying people to Washington: school buses like our own with signs taped on them saying, "Freedom Now"; chartered cruisers; even a dilapidated old city bus with a sign saying, "We Shall Overcome." As each bus passed, the people on board leaned out of the windows and let out a scream of recognition when they saw us.

Everyone who wasn't already standing rose to his or her feet in salute. "Hooray!" we called back to them, raising our arms in the air.

"I've never seen anything like it," Frieda said, shaking her head slowly.

"Exciting," my mother said, taking my hand in hers. "Very exciting!"

All of us remained standing, looking out toward the highway. The great group of buses had disappeared, but every few minutes one or two more buses passed, many of them stating on handwritten signs their places of origin.

"Burlington, Vermont," I called out. "Brooklyn, New York. Albany, New York. Hartford, Connecticut," I yelled.

"Manchester, New Hampshire. Boston, Massachusetts," Ruthie yelled. "Newark, New Jersey."

It was clear that many of the cars whooshing past us were carrying demonstrators as well. As they sped by, we could see the outline of too many people squeezed into each car.

"Why are we standing here?" I asked, excited. People were starting to board the bus.

"Let's go!" Charlayne grabbed my hand and ran laughing with me to the bus.

Behind us, Janet and Ruthie, my mom and Frieda followed. We all felt silly, as if we'd had something fizzy to drink. In four or five minutes we were all aboard the two buses and on the final leg of the journey to Washington.

17

"Look at that," Janet said, pointing out the window. The bus was crawling up a Washington, D.C., street called New York Avenue in the middle of heavy traffic. Trailers, cars, bicycles, buses, and station wagons inched their way toward the demonstration.

"Look at what?" I asked.

"Over there. On roller skates," Janet said. "Charlie. Ruthie. Look at that guy!"

At the edge of the avenue, a man skated along wearing a large sign that said, "Going to Washington, D.C., for Civil Rights."

"You don't think he skated all the way here, do you?" I asked.

"Looks that way," Janet answered.

I stuck my head through the half-opened window and watched as he carefully wove his way between cars and buses. People tooted their horns and leaned out of their cars to wave and salute him.

"Attention," someone in the front of the bus said. "Attention, please." A Negro man in a shiny dark suit looked down the aisle at us. "It is now twelve forty-five p.m. In a few minutes, we will be dropping you off. I'm afraid we've missed the march from the Washington Monument." The motor of the bus sputtered and everyone sighed in disappointment. "However, we will be just in time, perhaps only a tiny bit late, for the demonstration at the foot of the Lincoln Memorial. Traffic is banned today in part of the city, but we will try nevertheless to get you as close as possible to the demonstration. Good luck to you all. We shall overcome!"

Everyone applauded and people began to move about, stretching their legs and assembling their belongings in anticipation.

A few blocks up the avenue, the bus made a turn and in another few minutes slowed to a stop and opened its doors. I stood up, trembling with excitement, and followed Frieda and my mother down the aisle and out the door.

The streets were filled with people. Frieda, my mother, Janet, Charlie, Ruthie, and I clung together and let the crowd jostle and move us along with it in the general direction of the Lincoln Memorial. Not a one of us had any idea where we were or how to get where we were going, but it didn't seem to matter; it was as if we and everyone around us were all tiny specks of metal and the Lincoln Memorial a magnet, drawing us slowly and inexorably toward it. With one hand I clutched the back of Janet's shirt and with the other my mother's elbow. One way or another, we were all connected, Charlie holding on to Frieda, Frieda holding on to Ruthie, Ruthie holding on to Janet. After a few minutes, the crowd loosened up and we were able to walk freely. In the distance I could hear the sound of someone singing and playing a guitar. Far behind me a huge arrowlike statue pointed skyward. Alongside us a long flat pool of water mirrored the statue. It all looked vaguely familiar.

"What's that pencil thing?" I asked.

"The Washington Monument," Frieda answered.

"And the water?"

"The Reflecting Pool," Janet said with excitement. "I've seen photos of all this. Picture postcards."

"Where's the Lincoln Memorial?"

"Up ahead."

I raised my eyes, looked past the small sea of people in front of us, and caught a glimpse of a white marble colonnade gleaming in the midday sun. A speaker's platform had been erected on it and several dark dots were moving across it. The music, which got louder as we got closer, was coming from loudspeakers on the platform.

"I can't see a thing," I complained.

"Frieda brought her binoculars," Janet said.

"And we'll get closer," Frieda said with determination. "We just have to stick together." Seizing my mother's hand, she led us forward, politely but firmly pushing her way past all kinds of people, most of them black but a good number of them white, some of them young, some old, and some middle-aged. After a good ten minutes, we reached the thickest part of the crowd. From there to the foot of the Memorial, people were packed in solid.

"I'm afraid this is the best I can do." Frieda sighed with disappointment.

"It's fine," my mother reassured her.

I stood on tiptoe and squinted. I could just make out a handsome, heavyset Negro woman who was playing the guitar.

> Come go with me to that land,
> Come go with me to that land,
> Come go with me to that land
> Where I'm bound. . . .

"It's Odetta," I yelled, recognizing her more by her voice than by what little I could see of her.

"Really?" Charlayne jumped into the air and craned her neck to look over the crowd. "Wow!" she said when she landed.

Around us people were still milling about and getting settled. The whole thing felt more like a carnival than a demonstration. Folks were talking, singing, and clapping along with Odetta. The sun beat steadily down on all of us. Frieda opened a small knapsack and removed eight folded sailor hats. "Wear them," she commanded, handing the two extras to a middle-aged couple standing near us and carrying a sign that said, "Methodists Mean Business. Equal Rights Now!"

"Buttons! Twenty-five cents! Get your buttons!" a young boy hawked. He carried a felt board filled with hundreds of round buttons showing a white hand clasping a black hand. "Money goes to the movement!" he shouted.

"Over here," Ruthie called, pulling a dollar out of her pocket. "Four," she said to the kid. "My treat."

"Thanks," Janet, Charlie, and I said, pulling them off the board.

"And two for the old ladies," my mother said, handing the boy fifty cents.

On the speaker's stand, they were introducing another singer, but it was hard to hear who it was. Janet peered through the binoculars. "Joan Baez," she announced, shaking her head from side to side. "Joan Baez." I grabbed the binoculars away from her and peered through them. There on the other side of the glass, as real as anybody, was Joan Baez, her long black hair sliding across her shoulders and the clear bell-like voice coming from her lips. She looked up and it was as if she were singing directly to me.

> We shall overcome.
> We shall overcome.
> We shall over . . . ©

I passed Charlayne the binoculars and joined in.

More and more people had gathered, and we were now in the middle of the crowd rather than at the back. There were people as far as I could see, in front of us, alongside us, behind us, lining the edge of the Reflecting Pool. Everyone was, for the most part, dressed as conservatively as we were—the men in business suits, the women in dresses or skirts and blouses. Many of them carried signs or placards saying, "No More Segregation," "With Liberty and Justice for All," "Freedom Now." Here and there a young child stood in the crowd, but it seemed that most people were there as if on business and had left their children behind.

Above us a helicopter bobbed and swooped down like a giant dragonfly investigating the scene. Photographers leaned into the crowd, snapping pictures or filming us. Nearby, a group of about ten Negro boys wearing white sweat shirts and black armbands had gathered.

"What are the mourning bands for?" Charlayne asked one of them.

"Injustice in America," he answered.

Charlayne nodded her silent approval and turned back toward the speaker's platform. The singing had ended and someone was being introduced. Around me, people seemed to come to attention.

"What are they saying? Who is it?" I asked.

"A rabbi from the American Jewish Congress. Rabbi Jordan Prince," Charlayne answered.

"Rabbi *Joachim Prinz,*" Frieda corrected, smiling.

"I wish I could sing," the rabbi said, and everyone laughed. "I speak to you as an American Jew," he said, pronouncing the words in an accent that sounded part English and part European. "As Americans . . . we share the profound concern of millions . . . of people . . . about the shame and disgrace of inequality . . . and injustice which makes a mockery of the great American idea. As Jews, we bring to the great demonstration in which thousands of us proudly participate a . . ."

It was hot and difficult to concentrate. I watched Charlayne as she stood alongside me listening. The tendons in her neck were taut and straight as she strained to hear what the rabbi was saying.

"Friends, I was the rabbi of the Jewish community in Berlin under the Hitler regime . . . I learned many things, the most important thing that I learned in my life . . . and under those tragic circumstances . . . is . . . that bigotry and hatred are not the most urgent problems. The most urgent . . . the most disgraceful . . . the most shameful . . . and the most tragic problem is . . . silence. . . ."

"Hear! Hear!" someone on the speaker's stand shouted, and suddenly I and everyone else wanted to applaud.

". . . A great people which has created a great . . . civilization has become a nation of onlookers. . . ."

Even though I didn't know the rabbi who was speaking, I felt connected to him, almost as if he were a relative of mine. In a way, he was. We shared the same religion, and it was this kind of religion—the reaching-out kind—that made me proud to be Jewish. Using your own particular experience to reach beyond yourself and help other people was what I felt religion should be all about.

I thought about some of the people at PROJECT who saw only the differences between people and were so frightened of those differences that they wanted to wall themselves in. I wanted to be like the rabbi, able to stir people and move them beyond themselves and their fears, the way I'd had to forcibly move myself beyond my own fears. When I was a lawyer, I'd do that. Maybe I'd start next year when I was PROJECT vice-president. *If* they elected me.

The rabbi's speech ended and everyone applauded enthusiastically. The sun, like a glowing chunk of coal, burned bright orange in the sky. The whole world seemed to be steaming. I removed my sailor hat and wiped the perspiration away. "It's hot," I breathed to no one in particular.

Janet smiled and opened a large red Thermos. "Here," she said.

I took the Thermos and sipped sweet, cold lemonade. "Thanks," I sighed, passing it to Charlayne. "You and Frieda think of everything."

Bob Dylan was singing a song about the murder of Medgar Evers. He seemed to spit out each and every word.

"He looks frail," my mother said, looking through the binoculars. "And he can barely sing. Do you think he's ill?"

"No," I said, feeling great love for her. "It's just his style."

She nodded as if she were filing this information for the future and passed the binoculars to Ruthie.

I raised my eyes and looked at the fat, round, leafy trees that ran along the sides of the Reflecting Pool. Here and there, in an attempt to get a better view of the proceedings, a human being dangled from a branch like an exotic fruit.

It was after two and the heat was becoming more and more

intense. I squinted and peered out from behind my lashes. I could almost see the hot vapors rising vertically from the ground. Soon I was off in a kind of trance state as one speaker after another took the podium and addressed the enormous crowd. Scattered phrases floated toward me across the hot air as if in a dream. ". . . to be as brave as our sit-ins and our marchers, to be as daring as James Meredith, to be as unafraid as . . ." Somewhere a bird called out, and off in the distance I heard the sound of applause. ". . . demand that segregation be ended in every school district in the year 1963 . . ." Someone cheered. ". . . enact civil-rights legislation now . . ." People applauded. " . . . have the pleasure to present to you, Dr. Martin Luther King, Jr." Martin Luther. Martin Luther. King. Martin Luther Betsy. Martin Luther Betsy.

"Wake up. Wake up, Betsy." I opened my eyes. My mother was shaking me, and Frieda, Janet, Charlie, and Ruthie were staring at me with concern. All around me was the sound of huge applause.

"Are you okay?" my mother asked. Janet handed me what was left of the lemonade.

"Yes," I said, gulping it down and slowly coming to. "The heat . . . Oh, no! Did I miss everything?"

"No, you're just in time. Listen!" Charlayne said, her face bright with excitement.

People were chanting, "Martin Luther King. Martin Luther King. Martin Luther King." Over and over again the chant continued. And as it did, signs and placards bobbed up and down like white ducks on a dark sea. Women waved handkerchiefs and some people cheered. I stood on tiptoe and stretched my body longer than I'd ever before stretched it. There in the distance on the speaker's stand, seemingly in miniature, was the round, brown face of Martin Luther King. A small electric charge shot up the back of my spine.

Gradually the shouting and chanting and applause died down and I realized that Dr. King had already begun his speech. ". . . today in what will go down in history as the greatest demonstration for freedom in the history of our nation . . ." I listened to the sound of his voice. It was smooth and warm—the voice of a patient, caring minister. He spoke about how one hundred years ago Abraham Lincoln had signed the Emancipation Proclamation and how the Negro was still not free. That today Negroes were still the poor and the exiled in affluent America. He spoke about how America had given the Negro people "a bad check" and how now they were ready to demand their rights to equal opportunity and justice.

". . . We can never be satisfied as long as our children are stripped of their selfhood and robbed of their dignity by signs saying 'For Whites Only' . . . We cannot be satisfied as long as a Negro in Mississippi cannot vote and a Negro in New York believes he has nothing for which to vote. No, no, we are not satisfied, and we will not be satisfied until justice rolls down like waters and righteousness like a mighty stream. . . ."

"Yes!" a woman on the speaker's stand shouted. Near us, the group of boys with the mourning bands whistled, and I and thousands of other people applauded. Above, an airplane's motor temporarily blocked out the sound of Dr. King's words. But then his calm, determined, almost relentless voice became audible again.

". . . Go back to Mississippi, go back to Alabama, go back to South Carolina, go back to Georgia, go back to Louisiana, go back to the slums and ghettos of our northern cities, knowing that somehow this situation can and will be changed. Let us not wallow in the valley of despair.

"I say to you today, my friends, so even though we face the difficulties of today and tomorrow . . . I still have a dream. It is a dream deeply rooted in the American dream. I have a dream that one day . . ."

"Yes!" the woman on the stand shouted again.

". . . this nation will rise up and live out the true meaning of its creed: 'We hold these truths to be self-evident; that all men are created equal.' "

"Hooray!" I yelled. I was clapping so hard, my palms hurt. Charlayne looked at me and smiled.

"I have a dream that one day in the red hills of Georgia, the sons of former slaves and the sons of former slave owners will be able to sit down together at the table of brotherhood. I have a dream—"

The applause that interrupted him was thunderous. The entire crowd was swept up in a surge of intense feeling. Dr. King kept calling out, "I have a dream," and describing a world in which Negroes and whites were equal. With each thing he said, the feeling became bigger and more intense.

Charlayne and Ruthie and Janet and Frieda and my mom cheered, their faces tilted toward the sky. And Martin Luther King's strong voice cried out inexorably now, both singing to us and calling to us.

". . . So let freedom ring . . . from the prodigious hilltops of New Hampshire. . . . So let freedom ring . . . from the mighty mountains of New York. Let freedom ring . . . from the heightening Alleghenies of Pennsylvania! Let freedom ring from the snowcapped Rockies of Colorado! Let freedom ring from the curvaceous slopes of California!"

"Yes, sir!" someone behind me shouted.

"But not only that; let freedom ring from Stone Mountain of Georgia! Let freedom ring from Lookout Mountain of Tennessee. Let freedom ring from every hill and molehill of Mississippi. From *every* mountainside, let freedom ring. . . ."

My body trembled. I felt as if my insides were about to reverse themselves and burst outward. And still Dr. King's voice and words continued building to a crescendo.

"And when this happens, when we allow freedom [to] ring, when we let it ring from every village and every hamlet, from every state and every city, we will be able to speed up that day when *all* of God's children, black men and white men, Jews and Gentiles, Protestants and Catholics, will be able to join hands and sing in the words of the old Negro spiritual, 'Free at last! Free at last! Thank God Almighty, we are free at last!' "

It was the end of his speech. I was crying, and when I looked around me, I saw that, though everyone smiled, nearly all of us were simultaneously crying. My mom, Frieda, Charlie, Ruthie,

Janet, and I reached for each other and hugged in one huge, flailing embrace. When we finally pulled apart, the applause around us was like a crash of thunder.

A Negro woman behind me kissed me on the cheek and smiled. I looked left and right and forward and back, and all around me wherever I looked, whether at someone with black skin or with white, I saw one huge smiling family. It would be that way for real one day. I believed it in my bones. In twenty or thirty years, when my own children were my age, they and their Negro friends would be neighbors and equals. There would be no need for demonstrations. There would be no need for protests or for acts of Congress. The world would be a family of men and women and it wouldn't matter what your religion was or whether your skin was white, black, brown, yellow, red, or purple, we would all be brothers and sisters.

Marian Anderson's deep, rich voice sang out the words to "He's Got the Whole World in His Hands," and as I held hands with Charlie and Janet, I had no doubt at all that I was right.

About the Author

RONI SCHOTTER is both a writer and a children's book editor. Her writing has appeared in several literary magazines and she is a member of the Bank Street Writers' Lab and the Writers' Community. Her first novel, *A Matter of Time,* was made into an Emmy Award-winning "ABC Afterschool Special."

Ms. Schotter was born in New York and grew up in Providence and Pawtucket, Rhode Island. She was educated at Carnegie-Mellon University and New York University where she received a B. A. in English. Ms. Schotter now lives in New York City with her husband Richard, who is a playwright, and their young son, Jesse.